Conan charged into their midst, laying about him with the flat of his sword. "Stand and fight, you puke-blooded cowards!" he roared. "Where will you hide? Stand and fight—or die!"

Despite their panic, the Cimmerian's presence overawed them. For a moment there was hesitation.

"Follow me, you gutless dogs!" Conan railed at them. "Back to the barricades! We can hold Korst's butchers! He's been driven back from every other front! Stand and fight, I tell you! Let them overrun us here, and we're all of us dead men! Follow me!"

Without looking back to see if they obeyed him, Conan rode through them—intending to fight alone to the death rather than die with cowards.

Chronological order of the CONAN series:

Illustrated CONAN novels:

Other CONAN novels:

CONAN

16

THE ROAD OF KINGS

Karl Edward Wagner

ACE BOOKS, NEW YORK

FOR LEIGH BRACKETT

And the song of Shannach ebbed into silence, as the last of the children of mountains went forever into night.

This Ace book contains the complete text of the original edition. It has been completely reset in a typeface designed for easy reading, and was printed from new film.

CONAN THE ROAD OF KINGS

An Ace Book / published by arrangement with
Conan Properties, Inc.

PRINTING HISTORY
Bantam edition / October 1979
Ace edition / December 1987

ISBN: 0-441-11618-3

Ace Books are published by The Berkley Publishing Group,
200 Madison Avenue, New York, New York 10016.
The name "ACE" and the "A" logo
are trademarks belonging to Charter Communications, Inc.

PRINTED IN THE UNITED STATES OF AMERICA

10 9 8 7 6 5 4 3 2 1

Contents

War is father of all things, king of all things; it makes of some men gods, of some free men, and of others slaves.

—HERACLITUS

Prologue

Frozen stillness, and diamond-bright steel.

Two swords shimmered in the smoky light, ringed by a faceless circle of eyes no less pitiless and bright. A shiver of motion, and the blades clashed together—shattering the stillness with the clangour of angry steel. Then, explosive grunts and gusts of breath, wrenched from the sweaty throats of the two combatants. A hoarse rush of breath and subdued murmur from the circle of watchers; faceless eyes glinted with excitement. Then blade again confronted blade: death balanced on striking steel; patient, remorseless.

The two men who fought here shared little in common other than the deadly skill with which each wielded his blade.

One, who was increasingly on the aggressive, was clearly the older man, and his dexterous swordplay indicated that the long, straight Zingaran blade was no stranger to his fist. Bars of gray highlighted his smooth black hair and closely trimmed beard, even as his handsome face was streaked by a few straight duelling scars. The scars were thin and faded, for it had been many years since an opponent's blade had touched this face. Burgundy trunk hose and velvet doublet of finest quality set off a lean figure of compact muscle and confident poise. Emblazoned upon his right sleeve was a

1

black eagle—the insignia of Korst's Strikers, the elite regiment of the Zingaran army—and beneath that, the twin gold stars of a captain.

The other was a younger man—probably of no more than half the captain's forty-odd years. Withal, he parried his opponent's sword with a studied skill that was more of the veteran swordsman than the reckless youth. He was somewhat taller than the older man's six feet of height, and considerably heavier of build. Stripped to the waist, his powerful shoulders and broad chest showed a deep tan, its evenness flawed now and again by lines of scar—hallmarks of the battles and scrapes that had schooled his sword-arm. A sweaty mane of black hair whipped about his cleanshaven face as he fought; blue eyes smouldered angrily from his rough-hewn features. He wore the leather trousers of a northern barbarian, and his huge fist seemed better suited to a heavy broadsword than to the thin, double-edged Zingaran hand-and-a-half sword.

They stood within a circle of soldiers, tightly compressed to watch this duel. The majority of the onlookers wore the burgundy and gold colors of the Royal Zingaran Army, as well as the eagle insignia of Korst's Strikers. Shouldered together with them were men of other regiments, along with a scattering of warriors in mismatched and nondescript gear—soldiers of Zingara's mercenary companies, as was the youth. About them arose the shadowy enclosure of a military barracks—cots and equipment shoved back against the walls to make room.

Tense faces were strained upon the combatants; knowing eyes missed nothing of the swordplay. Earlier the barracks had resounded with cheers and shouts, with the frantic exchange of wagers and curses. But that was before the two duellists had unleashed a heart-stopping display of slash and thrust, parry and counterthrust. Now the excitement was too intense for vocal expression. Sharing the tension of the duel, the onlookers hung to each breath and waited—even as the two combatants drew upon their limits of endurance and watched for the other to make his own fatal mistake.

Both of the bastard duelling swords had lately tasted blood. A shallow gash of no consequence leaked across the older man's forearm, where the other's blade had glanced from his cross guard in a blow that all but tore the hilt from his grasp. But the youth bled from a pair of slashes along his left side, and a deeper wound below his shoulder seemed to have crippled his left arm—stigmata of three deadly thrusts that would have pierced his heart had his reflexes been a fraction of a second slower. Perhaps this leeching flow of blood prompted the thin smile and flared nostrils of the older man, as he pressed confidently for the kill. The youth did not smile, and the wrath in his eyes blazed without hint of the pain and fatigue he must feel.

Again their blades darted, engaged, broke apart. Not pausing in his attack, the captain struck again, even as their swords disengaged—letting the impetus of their exchange drive his blade down and around the other's guard, stabbing deep into the thick muscles of his thigh.

The youth grunted in agony, lunging backward from the blow. His leg buckled under him. He staggered, barely holding himself erect. His desperate counterthrust was clumsy and without strength.

It was the final moment of the long duel. The circle of eyes burned with breathless concentration. Savouring the split-second of their absolute attention, the officer chose to dispatch his crippled opponent with the blinding thrust to the heart that was his trademark.

The youth had no thought of good form. From his half-crouch, he slashed upward—gripping the long hilt with the fingers of his wounded left arm for added strength. The end of the blade caught the older man in his crotch and continued upward. Poised to deliver his *coup de maître*, the captain was flung back in a welter of spilling entrails and burst lung.

A long gasp of disbelief, then a confused outburst of exclamations.

A man with glazing eyes stared up at them from the barracks floor. A youth with smouldering eyes glared back at them, as he slumped from the weight of his wounds.

For a heartbeat the tableau held.

Then the man on the floor shuddered in a final spasm—his death rattle drowned out in a sudden tumult of excited shouts and curses, rumble of jostled bodies and clink of coins. The youth put the bloody point of his sword to the floor, leaning hard against its hilt. Bright blood gushed from his thigh, but he made no outcry other than a hoarse gulping for breath.

He swayed on his feet; knuckles white upon swordhilt—as his strength drained from him. A pair of fellow mercenaries—almoners bursting with the coins they had just won—rushed forward to give him their shoulders. The youth's eyes blazed wildly—the battle-lust was still in his heart—then subsided as he recognized his comrades. He sagged against them, as a third soldier produced a strip of cloth bandage and worked to staunch the flow of blood from his thigh.

The uproar abruptly shivered to a hush. Soldiers hastily settled their wagers, anxiously sidled toward the doorways. A low murmur passed through the barracks:

"General Korst!"

The youth lifted his head and glowered truculently as the circle broke apart.

Followed by a number of his officers, the supreme commander of the Royal Zingaran Army, General Korst himself, swept into the barracks. A short, stocky man, Korst's blue-black hair and swarthy complexion betokened the admixture

4

of Shemite blood with that of his Zingaran father. That the son of a camp whore and an unknown Zingaran soldier should rise to generalship of class-conscious Zingara's army was a significant tribute to Korst's abilities.

The general's eyes widened, then narrowed, as he studied the disembowelled corpse. He stroked his carefully trimmed beard thoughtfully.

"Ah, Captain Rinnova! Then did you at last cross steel with one who was more than your match? *His* was not a stroke to the heart, it is true, but you're dead enough for all its crudeness."

He looked toward the wounded youth. Under the general's impassive gaze, those who held him sought to draw back. The youth swayed on his feet, as his friends melted away, but he managed to hold himself erect and to return the stare.

"Yours was the blade that gutted Captain Rinnova?"

"I killed him, true enough," the other growled in answer. "And in a fair fight. Ask any man here."

General Korst nodded. "It is hard to believe that any man could cross blades with Captain Rinnova and live to boast of it—let alone some barbarian mercenary. But the evidence is plain for all to see, as you have said. What is your name?"

"Conan."

"From the lands of the northern barbarians, I judge?"

"I am a Cimmerian."

"How are his wounds?" This to Conan's comrades, who were nervously seeking to slip into the background.

"Those cuts on his ribs are shallow; his arm is cleanly pierced. He's lost much blood from the wound in his thigh, but the blade missed the great artery there."

"Good." General Korst nodded to his men. "Then he'll live to hang. Whatever your quarrel, Conan of Cimmeria, a mercenary soldier is not permitted to butcher an officer

5

of the Royal Zingaran Army.''

Conan roared, staggered toward Korst—as his Strikers leaped between.

He managed to kill two of them—before the pack closed over him, clubbed him to unconsciousness.

''A waste of a good man,'' Korst pronounced, as they dragged Conan away. ''But these barbarians must be taught discipline.''

I. The Dancing Floor

The morning sun was bright—too bright for eyes that had looked upon no light save the torches of the prison guards for days unnumbered. A gray morning would have been kinder, but this was not a morning for kindness. The line of condemned prisoners pressed their eyes shut against the painful glare, stumbled blindly forward to the waiting scaffold. By the time they had crossed the prison yard, they were able to see the dangling nooses and the exuberant mob of onlookers.

Conan squinted toward the gibbet, a black line against the climbing sun, seven coils of hemp trailing like sooty cobweb from the span overhead. To his nostrils came the acrid sweetness of carrion—wafted from the rotting corpses of last week's condemned criminals, left to swing above the scaffold until seven new partners were brought to dance with death. It melded with the sweaty stench of the crowd's anticipation.

A halbard spike dug into his back. "Get on there, ravenbait!" growled one of the prison guards.

Conan snarled an obscenity and shuffled forward. Unkempt and unshaven, hobbled by the heavy chains that shackled his wrists and ankles, the Cimmerian nonetheless walked without a limp. A month in Kordava's dungeons

7

had seen his wounds slowly heal, although that was due far more to his savage vitality than to any ministrations of his warders. That same vitality had brought him through the degradation of his captivity with spirit unbroken, head unbowed.

Like a captured wild thing, Conan had licked his wounds and awaited his chance to break free of his cage. Stealthily, so that the rasp should not alert his guards, he had crouched throughout the night hours rubbing the links of his fetters one against the other, scraping them against the stone, striving to break free of the heavy chains that shackled hand and foot. Once free of his chains, there remained the iron bars of his cell, the vigilant guards beyond—these must be dealt with in their time. Conan only asked for a chance to win free, to avenge himself upon his captors—any chance, however slim. That chance had never come. Now, even as he and his fellow prisoners walked to the gibbet, the Cimmerian's angry gaze studied the crowded square, while his brain searched desperately for some last instant means to cheat the hangman.

The prison yard—the Dancing Floor, they called it here in Kordava—was rank with jostling humanity on this, the morning of market day. Each week they streamed into Zingara's capital city from the outlying towns and villages, to fill the marketplace with their wares and their cries: produce from the inland farms, merchandise from the city guilds, fish and exotic goods from the Western Ocean. What better way to add zest to a day of bargaining than the free spectacle of an execution on the Dancing Floor?

An undulating sea of massed bodies, peering faces—all eyes turned upon the seven doomed men who trudged through their press and toward the scaffold. Seven men, seemingly no different from the hundreds of their fellows who had come to enjoy their final moments. Seven to dance for them. The crowd was not hostile, but neither was it sympathetic. Its mood was one of expectancy, of impatience for the show to begin. The beast would not lift its thousand arms to wrest the condemned from their fate; if at all, it would howl in anger should its anticipated enjoyment be denied it.

Moving throughout the milling throng, peddlars and mountebanks hawked their wares. Less open in their larceny, thieves and cutpurses prowled like wary jackals. Portable braziers spat fumes from grilling skewers of meat and vegetables—reminding Conan that he had not eaten since the day before.

"We don't waste good food on gallowsbait!" a warder had sneered, as they came to his cell this morning. It had cost the guard a broken tooth when they unshackled Conan from the wall.

Halbard butts had quickly drubbed the Cimmerian to unconsciousness. "For that," promised the warder, spitting bloody froth into Conan's battered face, "you get to wait to the last! You'll watch these other rats kick on their strings, and then we'll hoist you nice and easy, so you can show us all the new steps you'll have learned from your fellows."

It was, withal, a certain victory for the Cimmerian. The other prisoners had their manacles removed, their wrists pulled behind their backs and tied with rope. Wary of the powerful barbarian's berserk frenzy, the guards were loath to risk removing his prison shackles, so that Conan walked to the gallows in chains.

With a barbarian's stoicism, Conan resigned himself to die with dignity—if die he must. He would march to the scaffold, if the alternative was to be dragged. That his belly growled from hunger pains as he walked to his death was but one final insult after many before it, and the Cimmerian swore vengeance in that hour when most men would be begging their gods for forgiveness and mercy.

The stench of carrion was heavier now. Stiffly sprawled

before the scaffold, seven corpses stared heavenward through eyeless sockets. Rooks had feasted well upon their features, obliterating recognition. Their week-long sentence as object lesson to fellow miscreants now fulfilled, the dead had been lowered from their nooses, laid out for a last farewell to the crowd. Laborers dragged them one by one to a small anvil, where the leg shackles of the dead were struck off. They had no further need for them, and there were others whose steps wanted confining.

By royal concession, mountebanks peddled charms and souvenirs from the hanged men. A pack of children struggled and giggled about the scaffold, pressing closer for a better look.

"Lock of dead man's hair for you, lasses?" teased a hawker, yanking a tuft loose and dangling it before them. "It'll keep the lads following after you, if you pin it over your heart!"

With shrill laughter the children dashed away, began to play a darting game of tag beneath the scaffold timbers.

"Dead man's hand! Who'll be first to buy?" A stroke of the axe, and the trophy came free. "Hand of a hanged murderer!" the mountebank shouted, holding the decaying fist on high. "Corpse-fat for candles! Do you seek hidden treasure? Here's the charm you'll need! Who will pay me silver to find gold?"

"Seed of a dead man!" cried another, brandishing a small phial. "The death-spend of Vulosis, the famous murderer-rapist! Men! The vitality of a young stallion is yours! Ladies! Restore your man to the ardour of a young bull! Hanged man's seed! Who will buy?"

Through it all, the key players of the morning's spectacle slowly made their way. Before the halbards of the guards, the mob broke apart to let them pass. A thousand faces craned and peered, examining the seven players in their costumes of rags and chains. Parents lifted children to their

10

shoulders for a better view. Shoulders, elbows and knees propelled latecomers through the press. They fed on skewers of meat and lumps of bread and fists of fruit. Their arms hugged their bundles and purses and baskets to their bodies. As the condemned men reached the scaffold, the frolicking band of children yelled and danced about them. Pedlars lost interest in their frenetic hawking, turned to watch the sordid drama they had seen performed so many times before.

Climbing the steps to the scaffold was no easy task with leg-irons, but the guards plied their halbards with a will to urge them upward. The man in front of Conan stumbled— unable to catch himself with his hands tied behind his back. A halbard spike goaded him as he struggled to rise. Conan, his hands manacled before him, reached out to the limit of the chain that connected wrist and leg-irons, caught the back of his jerkin and hauled the smaller man to his feet. Ignoring the abuse of the guards and the laughter of the crowd, they took their places beneath the gallows.

"Thanks," muttered his companion automatically. He seemed no more than Conan's age—a slender youth with aristocratic features and feverish dark eyes.

"Little cause for thanks," the Cimmerian pointed out.

"One likes to do these things with a certain dignity," returned the other, echoing Conan's thoughts. He nodded distastefully toward some of those near the head of their line: one man had fainted and had to be supported by the guards; another was pleading tearfully for mercy to the jeering mob.

"Let those who will continue our battle see that we do not tremble to give our life to our cause," he concluded. Conan wondered to whom these brave words were directed, decided the youth was but speaking to himself.

They stood upon a long scaffold, the faces of the crowd on a level below their feet. Massive uprights at either end supported a huge overhead beam—more than sturdy enough

11

to bear the weight of seven men. There was no trap to the scaffold. Instead, each waiting noose was passed through an overhead iron hook, with the other end of the rope secured to a windlass and rachet apparatus. No sudden drop and quick death from a broken neck here. This was the Dancing Floor, where the recipients of Zingaran justice were slowly hoisted from the scaffold and left to writhe and kick until strangled.

Passing along the row of the condemned, a warder solemnly hung a placard about the neck of each man. Pausing before Conan, he took care to stand clear of the Cimmerian's manacled hands.

Conan scowled down at the placard that lay upon his broad chest. He tried to spell out the inverted letters, but his ability to read Zingaran was dubious under any circumstances. "What does it say?" he asked his companion.

The thin youth glanced at the placard with ironic interest. "It says: *Conan Mutineer*. Congratualtions."

"What does yours say?" Conan wanted to know.

"Mine proclaims: *Santiddio Seditionary*. Our companions are sundry thieves, murderers and publishers."

"Publishers?"

"No, I wasn't merely being redundant. The fellow on the end there had the misfortune to publish my little political treatise that so incensed our beloved King Rimanendo."

"May your beloved king catch the pox from his catamites!" snarled Conan. "I killed an officer in a fair fight of his asking, and Rimanendo's laws declare that to be mutiny and murder!"

"Ah!" Santiddio's feverish eyes studied him with sudden respect. "Then you're that barbarian mercenary who gutted the dashing Captain Rinnova! Korst's chief butcher, that one. I'd shake your hand, if these ropes would permit it. The people will mourn the loss of two heroes of their struggle this day."

12

"Cut the chatter, you two!" a guard warned, as he fitted nooses about their necks. "You'll wish you'd saved that breath before long!"

The crowd didn't look mournful just now, Conan decided. Stoically he gazed out across the morass of bodies. Arguments and angry scuffles broke out as latecomers forced their way to the front of the crowd. Glancing down at their surly faces and rough clothes, Conan judged that many of these late arrivals could as easily be standing upon the gallows as amongst the throng. He wondered at the morbid curiosity that compelled them to watch the execution of their fellow brigands.

A cheer from the crowd broke off Conan's musings. Anonymous in his black mask, the king's executioner ascended the scaffold and returned the applause with a grandiose bow. Swaggering across the platform, he inspected the preparations of his assistants with the businesslike air of a director who surveys the stage and the players before lifting the curtain on his drama. His smile was polished, with just the right inflection of suave boredom. It was a professional touch that seemed to bestow confidence upon the players. Conan had seen that same smile on a day when the royal executioner had broken a man on the wheel.

A harsh rattle of the rachets brought Conan's gaze around—even as the hemp noose about his throat suddenly bit into his flesh. Under the royal executioner's supervision, the guards were completing final preparations—turning the seven windlasses so that each of the condemned prisoners stood straight upon his toes beneath the tautly stretched rope.

Beneath his outward impassivity, Conan's mind grappled with the hopelessness of his plight. Until this moment, he had been unable to accept the reality of his situation. Always there had been the false hope of escape, the lingering sense of outraged justice that argued that this could not be happening to him. Conan had faced death uncounted times since his childhood in the savage northlands. Always he had escaped; it bred for a certain contempt of death as an adversary. As the noose tightened about his neck, Conan fought down a rush of despair. Cimmerian warriors had died without a groan upon the torture stakes of the Picts, and Conan now stood straight and glowered his silent contempt upon the mob.

"In the name of his Royal Majesty, King Rimanendo," proclaimed the executioner above the vibration of the crowd, "let the sentences of his royal court be carried out!"

Abruptly there was silence, Conan sensed that the crowd was holding its breath—as was he. A dreamlike stillness seemed to grip those upon the scaffold.

Then the gnashing of the rachet's teeth, as the executioner cranked the first windlass. Neatly he coiled the hemp upon the horizontal barrel as it spun. Effortlessly, almost magically, the first of the condemned was levitated from the scaffold floor—to hang suspended beneath the gallows beam. Neck stretched impossibly, head twisted, eyes and tongue bulging from grimacing face, body writhing, leg-irons clattering: the first dance began.

There was a sighing murmur, then a rumble of harsh sounds—like surf soughing across sand to crash against the rocks. It was the chorus of the mob, letting out its breath and breaking into a babble of excited cries.

The second in line broke down then, shrieked mindlessly for mercy. The breath of the crowd smothered his sobs, and then came the laughter of the rachet wheel—as the noose lifted him toward the heavens that ignored him.

Tearing away from the morbid fascination that had bound his gaze upon the kicking puppets, Conan turned his face toward the crowd. Behind him, the executioner crawled like a great black spider upon its web—moving between the pieces of his apparatus, skillfully setting one rachet, then moving to the next windlass. Again the chatter of gears, and a third dancer twitched into the air.

Three more. And then . . .

But Hell was not waiting. Hell had come to the Dancing Floor.

Across the square—bawling howls of pain and terror, shrill trumpeting of panic-stricken horses. From one, then another, of the narrow streets that opened into the prison yard—billowing gouts of flame burst full into the screaming crowd.

Intent upon the hangman's inexorable approach, Conan's brain groped drunkenly to assimilate the sudden explosion of violence that erupted within the square. Two hay wagons, piled high with straw, spewed flame from out of the adjacent streets and into the packed square, as their fear-maddened teams tore into the ranks of onlookers. Black smoke boiled from the splashing streamers of yellow incandescence that engulfed both wagons—a glance told Conan that someone had thrown oil upon the hayracks before igniting them—as the blazing wagons ripped like vengeful comets into the horrified masses upon the Dancing Floor.

A glance impinged the flaming chaos upon his brain, but could not explain its sudden eruption. And as the stricken mob spun around from the gallows, to gape without comprehension upon the unforeseen terror that had burst upon them, another explosion of violence swept across the scaffold itself.

From the corner of his eye, Conan saw the blur of steel as it left the hand of one of those who had pushed to the foot of the scaffold only moments before. The hangman, poised beside the windlass of his fourth victim, straightened to gawk at the uproar across the square. The heavy-bladed throwing knife struck him full in the chest—its crimson haft a bursting flower upon his black velvet robe.

Carried back by the impact, the hangman maintained his death-grip upon the windlass crank. Death rattle and chatter of rachet blended, as the weight of his crumpling body spun the mechanism—wrenching the condemned man just beyond toes' reach of the scaffold. And King Rimanendo's royal executioner performed his office even as Death came for him.

Conan's gallowsmate was the first to recover from the paralysis of astonishment. "Mordermi! Mordermi!" he roared in glee. "Mordermi, you bloody bastard, I love you!"

"What's happening, Santiddio?" Conan demanded, as a riot broke out before the scaffold.

"It's Mordermi! These are Mordermi's men!" Santiddio yelled, struggling to slip his noose. "Sandokazi won him over!"

Conan knew Mordermi to be the boldest rogue among Kordava's not inconsiderable criminal populace, but the remainder of Santiddio's exultant outburst was beyond his comprehension. It was enough for Conan to understand that a desperate attempt to free the condemned prisoners was being made—albeit somewhat tardily—and the reasons behind such a move concerned him not.

The strangling noose bit into his throat. The hangman had previously taken in all slack in the ropes, so that his clients must stand on their toes to draw breath. It was a refinement that made it impossible for a frantic prisoner to duck out of his noose and make a futile leap into the crowd. Unless another hand freed him from the noose, Conan realized he could only stand helplessly beneath the gibbet while the melee raged about him.

Conan's wrists were chained in front of him, but the restraining length that connected manacles and leg-irons effectively prevented him from raising his hands above the level of his waist. Desperately Conan strained his powerful muscles in an effort to break one of the partially filed links of chain. His exertions were instantly halted by the noose, which all but throttled the Cimmerian into unconsciousness as he doggedly continued to strain against the heavy fetters.

Relaxing his muscles to gulp for breath, Conan took in the struggle within the prison yard. For a moment his vision blurred, throbbed agonizingly from the occluded circulation to his head. Beside him, Santiddio was dancing on his toes and howling like a madman—evidently a rescue did not demand the aloof dignity of an execution.

Across the square the mob surged and roiled in mindless panic to escape the frantic rush of the terrified draft horses and their juggernaut conflagration. Maddened by pain and fear, the teams could only plunge desperately forward— seeking to escape the blazing pyre that pursued them, heedless of the screaming masses of humanity that ripped apart beneath their smashing hooves. Made helpless by its panic-stricken myriads, the crowd flung itself to the outlying streets with all the blind impetus of a beheaded python—trampling scores of the less agile in its frenzy to escape. Blocked in by the press of the frantic mob, reinforcements from the prison itself were unable to force their way across the Dancing Floor.

Beneath the scaffold, Mordermi's brigands fought an uncertain battle with the guards who had been posted there for the execution. The initial surprise and confusion gave an advantage to the attackers—Conan judged there must be a score of them; in the chaos that ensued it was impossible to be certain. That any organized force would have the temerity, let alone the motive, to attempt to rescue any of these common felons from the public gallows was an eventuality that the prison officials would have deemed absurd. Now, as the beleaguered guards wielded their halbards in frantic defense against an unexpected assault, it would take time for a reserve force to breach the panic-stricken masses.

Backs to the scaffold, the remnant of the guard met sword and knife with their long-shafted halbards. Upon the scaffold itself: three bodies swung lazily, a fourth kicked frenetically

17

an inch above the platform, and the hangman's corpse glared at the three men who yet waited beneath their hempen tethers. The initial attack had cleared the scaffold of all others.

One of the attackers burst past the faltering circle of guards, dashed up the scaffold steps toward the helpless captives there. Santiddio shouted a cheer—then cursed impotently, as a halbard blade swept up out of the melee to sever their rescuer's leg at midcalf. Screaming, the crippled man pinwheeled back down the steps and into the struggle below.

"Santiddio!" Conan bellowed. "Stretch out your wrists toward me!"

Despite his excitement, the other man instantly understood. Turning his back to Conan, Santiddio extended his bound wrists toward the Cimmerian's manacled fists. By straining to the limits of their nooses, they were just able to bring their hands together. Setting his teeth against the throttling agony of the noose, Conan tore at the knots that held the other's wrists. The knots were hard, the cord tightly bound, cutting deep into Santiddio's wrists. Conan cursed and broke his nails digging against the knots. His temples throbbed with congested blood.

An angry shout penetrated Conan's consciousness for all his maniacal concentration on the knots: "Kill the prisoners! Kill the prisoners!"

Either to foil the escape attempt, or to cause the wouldbe rescuers to withdraw—the order had been given. Forcing his way out of the tumult below, a blood-spattered guard heaved himself onto the scaffold. An assailant from below seized the man's legs as they cleared the platform edge, tumbled onto the scaffold behind him. The guard dropped his halbard as they grappled. In a writhing heap, the two rolled across the timber planks—knives stabbing for flesh.

Conan clawed at the stubborn knots with bleeding nails,

18

finally loosening the tight cords. With a savage wrench, he dug his fingers into the loosened coils, tore the bonds away from the livid flesh.

Santiddio yelped, hastily flung off his loosened bonds. In another instant the slim youth was grasping the hempen rope, lifting himself clear of the scaffold. The slack he gained thereby took the tension from the noose, and after a frantic scramble, Santiddio slipped his noose and dropped back onto the platform.

"Free me!" Conan shouted. In the seconds that had elapsed, the guard had dispatched his opponent, and now stumbled toward them with lowered halbard. Santiddio could easily leap from the scaffold and disappear into the milling fray within the square. Conan would not have blamed the man—neither would he have forgiven him.

Instead Santiddio darted to Conan's side, turning his back on the swiftly advancing guard. "Just give me some slack!" he yelled.

Conan lifted himself onto his boot toes, as Santiddio wrestled to loosen the noose enough to slip it past the Cimmerian's chin.

The guard rushed past the third surviving prisoner, intent on impaling the freed Santiddio. The other condemned man lashed out his foot, tripped the unsuspecting guard. The guard staggered, whirled about—then drove his halbard spike through the helpless man's breast.

It gained them only a short breath of time, but that was enough for Santiddio to slip the hempen noose over Conan's jaw. Heedless of abraded skin, Conan dragged his head out of the noose.

In a frenzy, Santiddio flung himself against the guard—Conan thought of an alley cat attacking a coach dog—gripping the halbard shaft as the other yanked its spike free of the entrapping ribcage and spun to face him. Not troubling to break the smaller man's grip and bring the halbard blade

19

to play, the burly guard simply rolled over Santiddio—forcing him onto his back against the platform. Astride the youth's chest, the guard pressed the halbard shaft across Santiddio's throat—bearing down with killing pressure despite the other's frantic resistance.

Free of the noose, Conan was nonetheless far from a free man. Hobbled by his prison chains, he knew there was no chance to escape the circle of guards. Even as Santiddio went down, another guard was breaking away from the hard fighting at the scaffold steps to join his comrade in finishing off the prisoners.

Conan threw every ounce of his great strength against his iron fetters—bracing legs and shoulders to draw maximum tension upon the length of chain that joined wrist and ankle chains. Massive knots of muscle bunched upon naked torso and shoulders, strained against the confines of his tattered leather trousers. Iron cuffs gouged into wrists and ankles, grinding flesh against bone. Bright blood trickled from torn skin—at once diluted by the glistening sweat that poured from his straining flesh. The footsteps of the onrushing guard reached his brain but dimly through the sledging pulse of his heart.

Muscle against iron—one or the other must soon break under the unendurable stress. Iron was the weaker.

A link of the chain, eroded by hours of stealthy abrasion against its adjacent link, parted with a sudden wrenching. Conan's wrists were flung upward by the recoil—still chained together. To his disgust, Conan realized that only the connecting chain had parted—his wrists, his ankles were still fettered.

It was enough to save his life. As the second guard rushed upon his back, Conan whirled and sidestepped—swinging the length of chain between his wrists as if it were a flail. The chain snapped into the startled guard's face, ripping away his eyes and crushing the thin bone of the orbit. The

20

guard howled and plummeted from the scaffold.

With a quick leap, Conan was upon the other guard—too intent upon strangling Santiddio to recognize the sudden threat. In an instant, Conan had twisted his wrist chain about the guard's thick neck. Driving a knee into the man's back, Conan jerked savagely. The guard's head all but tore away from his smashed vertebrae.

Santiddio, face livid and gagging for breath, rolled out from under the halbard shaft. Conan dragged him to his feet, held him there until his knees grew steady. A quick look told Conan that the prison yard was emptying. A company of guards was pushing its way across the square through the thinning press of the mob. About the scaffold, the small remnant of their guards were concerned only with staying alive until reinforcements could relieve them, while their rescuers showed a growing inclination to withdraw and lose themselves in the fleeing crowd.

As the square began to clear, a small band of riders thundered their way against the flow of humanity. They led other mounts with saddles empty, and Conan saw that they were making for the gallows. Pounding hooves cleared a path through the dwindling crowd, as the mob had no thought save to take cover.

"It's Mordermi!" croaked Santiddio, still half-strangled. "Mitra! That's Sandokazi riding with him! They've brought us mounts! We're going to make it!"

"If they reach us before the guard regroups," Conan rumbled. He caught up the fallen halbard, shortened his grip on its shaft, and swung the blade between his legs with all his strength. The axe blade bit into the chain of his leg-irons. Striking with precision, Conan repeated the blow. The link parted, freeing his ankles.

Conan grunted in satisfaction. Grounding the weapon, he braced its butt between his feet, then pierced the halbard spike through one of the weakened links of his wrist chains.

Using leverage, Conan drew his arms back, twisting the chain link against the steel awl. For a moment it seemed that the spike would snap under the strain. Then the weld parted and the link twisted open.

With a harsh laugh, Conan waved his freed wrists, brandished the halbard. "Bring on your new hangman, you yapping pack of jackals! I'll hang him up by his own entrails!"

None of the guards remained to answer his challenge.

"Santiddio!"

Conan started. It was a woman's voice that hailed his comrade. Her hair a black banner beneath a red scarf, she rode at the head of the mounted band that plunged toward them, breaking past the fringes of the mob.

"Sandokazi! You did it!" Santiddio exulted, as they drew rein before the gallows.

"Hurry! The others will be on us in another moment! When the square clears, they'll not hesitate to use archers!" This from the leader of the horsemen—Conan took him to be Mordermi from the descriptions he'd heard of the infamous rogue. Mordermi took in the five dangling corpses and swore. "Mitra! I cut it close, my friend!"

"Come on, Conan!" Santiddio shouted. "We've a horse for you!"

The new force of guards was only moments away. Conan needed no second to the invitation. Vaulting onto the proffered saddle, he joined the tumultous charge back across the Dancing Floor and into the twisting streets beyond.

II.   The Pit

Although it had not been very many years since Conan had
wandered southward from the savage hills of his native
Cimmeria, he had experienced—and survived—more ad-
ventures than many a footloose rogue of twice his age. The
barbarian youth had visited many of the great cities of
the Hyborian kingdoms, and was no stranger to some of the
most notorious slums and criminal warrens that were found
there. He had been a thief in the Maul in Zamora, and there
learned the skills that had afterward made him one of the
most daring thieves in The Maze. But the Pit in Kordava
was unique among the many infamous thieves' dens that
blighted the major Hyborian cities.

In an earlier century, earthquake and fire had levelled
much of Kordava, with a portion of its waterfront sinking
beneath the sea. Preliminary tremors had caused most of
the populace to flee before the ensuing devastation, so that
many lives were spared. With tens of thousands left homeless
and Kordava in ruins, a new city was hastily raised upon
the broken body of the old one. Where destruction was
greatest, sections of Kordava were simply left buried beneath
the rubble—it being easier to fill over the devastation than
to haul away the rubble—and new streets and buildings
were erected upon the buried ruins.

Desperate in their need for shelter, many of Kordava's inhabitants had not waited for the new city to be built—instead had dug beneath the rubble, burrowing into the cellars and collapsed walls of the buried older city. The dangers of cave-in were balanced against the lure of free dwelling space and the prospect of recovering valuable loot from the buried debris. Tunnels were enlarged, the old streets uncovered and shored up, cellars and buildings dug out and vaulted over. As the years passed, and a new Kordava arose above the rubble, beneath its foundations the old city gnawed like a cancer—slowly being reborn as a subterranean warren for Kordava's impoverished and social outcasts.

From its earliest days, this district had been known as the Pit. The name was as suitable as it was inevitable. To the Pit settled the dregs of Kordava's populace: the poor and the misfit, the broken and the degenerate, those who preyed upon the mighty and the miserable. Criminals of all classes stalked the eternally shadowed streets brazenly; the city guard dared not enter the Pit, no more than could they have ferreted out their man in the labyrinthine ways of the buried city. Sailors on liberty and soldiers with their pay swaggered into the Pit in search of any sort of entertainment or vice their tastes might demand, for on the whole of the Western Ocean there were no waterfront dives with a notoriety more lurid than those of the Pit. It was said that in no pantheon was there a Hell peopled by demons and damned more depraved than those who dwelt within the Pit. Zingaran humor typically found a more scurrilous pun, equally appropriate. Conan had visited the Pit once during his brief career in the Zingaran army. That he had returned with no worse than a bad hangover and a purse depleted by his own free spending was no shoddy tribute.

Today Conan returned to the Pit boldly and upon a lathered horse, descending with his new companions along one of the numerous tunnels that led down to the buried streets of the old city. A hard ride from the area of the Dancing Floor had outdistanced any pursuit, and there were none in the crowded streets of market day to dispute their passage. Once returned to the Pit, a thousand of the guard might storm after Mordermi—and have less chance of taking him than of seizing laughter on the wind.

It was midmorning, so that wan pools of daylight filtered through skylights and airshafts overhead to augment the infrequent smears of streetlights. At this hour, the streets within the Pit were largely deserted, in contrast to those of the city above. For the Pit was a realm of night, just as its denizens were creatures of the night.

A few wine shops and brothels remained open; tired-faced whores loitered in their doorways, alert for any marketday rubes who might come early to sample the forbidden pleasures of the city. Streetlights, left burning in the perpetual gloom, shed their yellow light on only dirty pavement. Opium dens and gambling dives were boarded over upon the dreams of their addicts. Behind shuttered windows of the brothels, their inmates used their pallets for sleeping. Within clandestine little rooms, thieves and assassins slumbered with such pangs of conscience as they might feel. Outside the barred doorway of the vice den where Conan had seen her perform on stage with a Kushite dwarf, a six-year-old wearily poured slops into the gutter.

Architecturally—although such considerations were of little moment to Conan—the Pit was a living museum. An antiquarian would have noted with great enthusiasm the stuccoed façades and elaborate iron grillwork of another age, the ornate windows of stained glass and lozenge-paned streetlights that here and there had escaped destruction. Conan saw only filthy desolation and shabby efforts to patch together ruined structures that were better left to moulder. Skylights leaked barely enough daylight to break the gloom into varying depths of shadow. Airshafts did little to dispel the noxious miasma of smoke and decay and human misery.

A storey or more overhead, the omnipresent ceiling loomed like a sooty and starless firmament, shored up and vaulted over to support the world of daylight that moved unthinkingly above. Oddly truncated, the partially restored buildings of the old city were obliterated against the floor of the new city overhead. A subtle metastasis, some of these renovated structures opened into the cellars of the buildings of the new city; certain others masked cellars of their own that pierced to secret depths beneath the old. Foundation pilings from structures aboveground thrust downward in massive columns—like roots questing across the passage of a buried tomb. Indeed, the Pit was a catacomb, it seemed to Conan—a catacomb for the living.

Conan had spoken little with his companions throughout their ride. There had been no time for words during the wild gallop through Kordava's twisting streets and alleyways. Santiddio had vouched for him, after which Mordermi and the half-dozen of his men who rode with him had accepted Conan's presence without comment. Santiddio himself was too busy chattering with Sandokazi and Mordermi to spare Conan a thought. For the moment, Conan was content to put distance between himself and the slaughter upon the Dancing Floor. Clearly Santiddio was among friends here. The alliance of a high-minded intellectual and Kordava's most notorious outlaw was a puzzle that concerned Conan less than the matter of securing passage on the next vessel to sail for friendlier shores.

Ahead of them the street passed between a narrow corridor of shopfronts—from the boarded over windows and doorways, their aspect was one of long abandonment—and made a dead end against a brick wall. Mordermi and his men rode toward the barrier as if it were no more than a shadow across their path, so that Conan showed no surprise when a section of the wall slid downward into the earth to form an opening for their passage. As they rode past, the wall quickly rose back into place. Conan heard the faint grating of gears and counterweights as the hidden machinery functioned.

The wall, Conan decided, must once have enclosed the garden and ground of a wealthy estate. Beneath their horses' hooves, the tile mosaics showed dull visions of cavorting sea nymphs and dolphins through a patina of filth. Slabs of rubble paved the packed mud of flower beds, and a garden fountain was drowned beneath refuse. Brick supporting columns crowded in a forest of dank tree trunks to the vaulted ceiling where soot and nitre replaced clouds and stars. From somewhere close at hand came the iodine breath of the sea.

Beyond squatted the remains of what had been one of the old city's proudest mansions. Its massive walls reached two storeys or more to merge with the roof overhead; crude brickwork extended above the original stucco, and Conan guessed that this structure was one of those that arose innocently from the streets of the new city above. Lights shone from its diamond-paned windows, and cressets flared to disclose a great confusion of barrels, bales and mounds of stolen goods heaped about its walls and outbuildings.

A score of men, all heavily armed, lounged about the enclosure. More of their sort swaggered out of the mansion, shouting raucous greetings. Children came running from behind the brick pillars and broken statuary, yelling their excitement. A few slatterns leaned from the windows and hooted. Returning the applause, Mordermi and his men dismounted, turned the horses over to their fellows.

Conan followed suit, feeling the scrutiny of suspicious eyes.

Mordermi raised his arms in a grand gesture, shouting above the babble of questions.

"Your attention, gentle sirs! Your attention, please! As you know, I set out this bright morning to steal a gallows bird from King Rimanendo. Well, then. King Rimanendo was generous today—he's given me *two* gallows birds from his royal cages. Not only has he returned to us our learned brother, Santiddio, the very prince of polemicists . . .''

Here jeers and catcalls drowned him out. Santiddio made a sweeping bow.

"Not only Santiddio," Mordermi continued, "But our grateful king has presented us with the illustrious duellist and mutineer, Conan of Cimmeria, lately of Zingara's mercenary companies, and slaughterer of the unlamented Captain Rinnova!"

A heartbeat of silence as they absorbed Mordermi's grandiloquence—then boisterous cheers and applause. Men shouted congratulations, studied Conan with interest; a few came forward to pummel his shoulder and take his hand. Conan accepted their horseplay goodnaturedly; these were men of a breed he knew and liked.

A lithe rush of movement, and Sandokazi pressed against him. Her kiss was as warm as it was unexpected. Quickly again, she stepped away from him.

"I saw what you did there," Sandokazi told Conan. "Santiddio is my brother. I won't forget."

Then Mordermi was stepping between them. "Well now, Conan." His tone was light, but his smile was a little thin. "If you're through kissing my lady, why don't we see about knocking off all that iron jewellery you're carrying around."

III. The White Rose

A cloud of steam arose as the girl poured another kettle of boiling water into the bath water. Conan, wedged into the wooden tub and unable to evade the scalding water, cursed with his mouth full of wine and swatted at the wench with the chicken carcass he held in his other hand. The girl—Conan had already forgotten her name—laughed coarsely, and knelt to scrub his back with a sponge and the sulfurous-smelling soap that Santiddio swore would kill the prison lice. Her thin cotton shift, wet and clinging to her body, outlined a substantial physique. Conan, a tankard of wine in one fist and a carcass of half-cooked chicken in the other, suffered her ministrations with aplomb.

One of Modermi's men had struck off the Cimmerian chains. Now, in an oak-paneled chamber within Mordermi's lair, Conan and Santiddio tried to wash away the accumulated filth of their prison ordeal. Grinning whores attended them, and the steam-filled room took on the aspect of a public baths. Conan, impatient to fill his rumbling belly, saw no reason to delay his meal any further.

Santiddio, in the tub beside him, seemed neither hungry nor thirsty. Scrubbing briskly at his bony sides, he maintained an incessant stream of chatter, detailing the outrages of his arrest and imprisonment—evidently there had never been a trial—and of the struggle beneath the gallows. Mordermi listened politely, occasionally interjecting a question. Sandokazi, amusement in her dark eyes, paid more attention to Conan.

Seen beside her brother, the sibling resemblance was apparent. There were facial similarities in the angular chin, high-bridged nose, sensuous mouth, and glowing, almost over-large eyes. Sandokazi had the characteristic dark complexion of Zingarans, as well as heavy coils of lustrous black hair, haphazardly bound in a red scarf. She was as tall as her brother, slender and long-limbed. A well-developed figure was set off by her off-the-shoulder blouse of unbleached muslin, tight leather bodice, and wide, calf-length skirt of embroidered material. She was close enough to Santiddio's age, that Conan could not decide which was the elder.

Mordermi was younger than Conan had expected—probably not more than a few years his senior. He was a head shorter than the hulking Cimmerian as well, despite the high-heeled boots he chose to wear. The prince of Kordava's thieves had the reputation of being a dangerous opponent either in single combat or in a brawl, and Conan recognized the pantherish deadliness in the man's compactly muscled frame. He had a square jaw, and a nose that seemed to have been broken at least once. His face was alert; his dark eyes were piercing when he looked at you, veiled when you looked back.

Again, the dark Zingaran complexion, and an oily mass of black curls that he tied out of his eyes with a scarf that matched Sandokazi's. Conan considered the thin mustache and gold earrings a bit foppish, but then the fashions of Zingara were not to a Cimmerian's taste. In trunk hose and filigreed doublet of dark velvet, Mordermi might well be a prince of the blood, instead of prince of rogues. There was nothing effeminate about the double-edged rapier and quillon

30

dagger belted at Mordermi's trim waist.

Conan drained the tankard, and his buxom attendant made haste to refill it. The chicken was tough and poorly cooked, but Conan was too hungry to care. Luxuriating in the warm water, he gnawed with gusto at the stringy carcass, spitting the larger bones onto the floor. There were deep gouges along his wrists and ankles where the shackles had been struck away. Conan scowled at the marks and made a mental note to keep the sores covered until well healed—they were the telltale brand of a fugitive.

Mordermi's question indicated he had followed the Cimmerian's eyes and train of thought: "What will you do now, Conan?"

"Get out of Kordava," Conan answered. Beyond that much, he hadn't really given the matter thought. "Take passage on some ship, or maybe slip past the walls and into the hinterland, make for Aquilonia or Argos."

Mordermi shook his head. "No good. That's what they'll figure. They'll be watching the waterfront. Double guards along the city wall, and word will be speeding to the frontier. After that exercise on the Dancing Floor, Rimanendo will order Korst to recapture you two at any cost. Korst is no fool, and you're about as inconspicuous as a Vendhyan elephant in a dove's cage."

"All the more reason to get clear of Zingara," Conan agreed. "The Pictish Wilderness lies close beyond the Black River here, and chances are that Korst won't be watching *that* frontier too closely."

"With good reason," Mordermi agreed. "No white man has ever crossed the Pictish Wilderness."

"Do you want to tell a Cimmerian about Picts?" Conan wondered caustically.

Mordermi grinned at the gibe. "Why not stay here? You're as safe in the Pit as anywhere. Mitra, half of my men would be dancers if they strolled past the magistrates'

31

hall. Korst knows their faces and knows where to find them—but he dares not seek them in the Pit."

"After today?" Santiddio suggested. "We've ruined Rimanendo's digestion, be certain. I've often wondered whether he might move in force against the Pit if there were sufficient provocation."

"Well then, let him move against us. They can seal off a thousand exits; we can leave by a thousand more. Let them search through a thousand cellars; we'll laugh at them from a thousand undreamed of coverts. If I know Korst, he'll hire assassins to seek you out, and consider his responsibility in the matter to be delegated. Assassins we can deal with. Are you worried about assassins, Conan?"

Conan bit the head off of the chicken carcass, laughed over a mouthful of crunching bones.

Mordermi grunted. "Well, this is it then. Stay here while Rimanendo's fools wait for you to escape. I know men. I saw what you can do there on the scaffold. And any man who could kill Rinnova in a fair duel has more to him than just guts and muscle. I can use you, Conan. My men and I live pretty well, as you can see, and I see to it that every man gets a fair share. You'll make a damn sight better pay with me than as a mercenary, and the risks are about the same. Give things a little time to cool off—then if you want to show your heels to Kordava, you can do it loaded down with gold."

"Softly, Mordermi!" Santiddio protested. He was vigorously towelling his lean frame. "You forget that Conan is not just another of your common thugs. He's a man of natural principles and a political prisoner, as was I."

"A barbarian mercenary . . . ?" Mordermi started to protest.

"And a man of native honor may entertain understandable scruples at the invitation to join a gang of thieves," Santiddio shouted him down. "Conan, you should know that our

32

motives are the highest. We are not bandits; we are altruists.''

"Santiddio, I don't think Conan . . .''

"Enough, Mordermi! Your rescue this morning—an undertaking which, I will point out, entailed enormous risk and not one copper of profit for you—clearly proves that you *are* one of us. Conan, you have, of course, heard of the White Rose.''

Conan, his mouth full of wine and chicken breast, had been looking toward Sandokazi for guidance. Her full lips sucked at an orange, but her eyes smiled amusement. Conan worked to swallow. *Was the White Rose that dive where . . .*

Santiddio liked the sound of his own words too much to require a reply. "As you know, the White Rose is the revolutionary army dedicated to the overthrow of King Rimanendo and his corrupt court, and to the establishment of a free republic of the Zingaran people. Doubtless you will have seen our broadsides—we circulate them faster than Rimanendo's stooges can tear them down. Or you may have read our leaflets, perhaps even my own most recent pamphlet—the one that led to our acquaintance under the gallows.''

Conan nodded politely, licking grease from his fingers. The chicken had taken enough of the edge from his appetite to restore his equanimity. He did vaguely recall some sort of furor in the barracks over the discovery of certain treasonous documents, some discussion of a secret society Rimanendo wanted rooted out. Such was a matter for the city guard to bother about, not for Zingara's mercenary companies, and Conan found political arguments as dull and fruitless as that other conversational exercise that so obsessed learned fools: religious discussions.

"Republic?'' Conan struggled with the unfamiliar Zingaran term. "What do you mean?''

"I'm not sure that your native tongue includes the concept," Santiddio said airily. "It is a creation of the most modern political thought. I don't know what you might call it—a commonwealth, perhaps, where people choose their rulers instead of accepting those the gods place over them. The idea is somewhat akin to the practices of certain primitive tribes who elect their chiefs."

Santiddio caught himself quickly. "Primitive meaning, in other words, ah, certain barbarian peoples . . ." He tried to recall in what manner the Cimmerians governed themselves.

"You said the White Rose was an army," Conan prompted. "Where are your soldiers?"

"The people of Zingara are our soldiers," Santiddio informed him, waving his arms to include the world. "For our cause is the cause of all men who seek freedom from the tyranny of a corrupt and willful despot."

Conan had been about to ask where their headquarters were, but now thought better of it. "And your officers? Who are they?"

"We have no officers—at least, not in the sense you mean," Santiddio hedged. "We have leaders, of course—but our leaders are men chosen by ourselves from our own ranks, not petty tyrants who secure their high position through wealth and birth."

"And who is the leader of the White Rose?" Conan persisted.

"Well, we have no *leader*—at least no one leader, per se; that is, no *one* person to whom all others are subservient. This is not to say that we are leaderless, of course."

Conan nodded, tankard poised halfway to his mouth.

"There are some, I suppose," Santiddio went on, "who would say that *I* am the leader of the White Rose. Of course, we do have our factions—any movement does. Certainly, Avvinti has his adherents among the conservatives, as does Carico with his muddy ideas on communal property. And there are others prominent in our movement who have a certain following.''

"Then who makes decisions?"

"Ah! We all do. We have discussions, form committees to study all aspects of the situation—then we vote on a course of action. The powers to command are held by all.''

Mordermi burst out laughing. "And if it had been left to your fellow florists, the ravens would be feasting on that glib tongue of yours, Santiddio. Do you know why the White Rose did nothing to secure your release? Because the committee designated to propose a rescue plan couldn't agree whether to storm the prison or to subvert your guards, while Avvinti maintained that you were far more valuable to the movement as a martyr than as a writer of half-baked political pamphlets.''

"That bastard, Avvinti! I'll kill him!" Santiddio flared. "But I thought Sandokazi has convinced you to throw your lot in with us.''

"Sandokazi was persuasive, I'll grant you—but the rescue today was entirely on my own initiative.''

"That bastard Avvinti!" Santiddio's face was murderous. "I'll give him his chance to earn a martyr's glory.''

Fuming, he struggled into the fresh garments Sandokazi had brought him. One of the whores made to help him with his trunk hose, but Santiddio impatiently brushed her away, hopped about the room cursing to himself.

Conan's attendant brought razor and mirror. She would have shaved him, but Conan didn't care to allow another hand to bring sharp steel that close to his throat. Letting her hold the mirror, he scraped at the growth of beard. Santiddio had no more than trimmed his own prison growth to its customary length.

"The situation in brief, Conan," Santiddio continued, as he busied himself tying his points, "is that Mordermi is in sympathy with the goals and principles of the White Rose, even though the conceited ass considers us little more than idealists and visionaries.''

"You and your friends *tell* the poor that the wealth of Rimanendo's court rightfully belongs to them," Mordermi said caustically. "I *take* those riches from Rimanendo's nobles and give them to the oppressed.''

"After exacting a profit.''

"I have my expenses to contend with, Santiddio dear. *You* are the one who speaks of altruism.''

"Mordermi!" Santiddio whirled to fix the outlaw with an accusing finger. "Beneath that cynical front beats a heart of stone. 'Kazi, where is my sword?''

Sandokazi spoke to one of the whores. The girl disappeared, returned shortly with a rapier in a slightly mildewed scabbard. Santiddio slid the double-edged blade from its scabbard, eyed it critically for a moment and made a few passes. Conan watched his movements with interest. Santiddio was quick with words; his talent was not confined to verbal fencing.

"Avvinti, it is time for a dialogue," Santiddio murmured, returning the blade to its sheath and belting it to his waist. "Conan, are you an oyster that you will soak in your shell all day?''

"Just bring me my clothes," Conan suggested.

"They crawled away," Sandokazi laughed. "The lice claimed them in the name of King Rimanendo, and carried them back to the prison for dessert. The girls are finding clothes to fit you.''

Conan handed the razor back to his doxy, washed the soap from his face. The water, he decided, had reached that point at which it was as likely to deposit dirt on his skin as wash it off, but at least he'd cleansed the stench of prison from his flesh. He climbed out of the tub, wrestled with the whore for the towel. Sandokazi watched him with ironic amusement, chewing at her orange.

By the time he had dried himself, they had brought fresh garments—clean, if not particularly new. Conan worked his legs into a pair of leather trousers, tight against his damp skin, and drew a loose-sleeved shirt of burgundy stuff over his head. His boots had been cleaned and hastily mended where the iron cuffs had gouged. There was a sleeveless houppelande, its brocade somewhat frayed, that made a snug fit across his chest—Conan suspected its original wearer had been a man of stout proportions—and a slouch-brimmed hat that Conan tried and discarded.

"Not bad," Santiddio judged. "You aren't going to be mistaken for one of Rimanendo's counts, but then again, you'll pass in a crowd."

Sandokazi laughed cynically.

"I'm sure we can obtain a more suitable costume, given time," Mordermi said smoothly. "Something a trifle more in the mode perhaps. After all, the guard will be looking for a ragged barbarian."

"I'll settle for a good sword," Conan told him.

"That much is easily done. Our arsenal is better stocked than our haberdashery here," Mordermi smiled. "A fine rapier perhaps? We have several to choose from as to edge and blade length. Or do you prefer the hand-and-a half sword with which you dispatched Captain Rinnova?"

"A broadsword would suit me better," Conan hazarded. He would have preferred the two-handed double-edged straight sword, but doubted that he would find one readily here.

"Of course," Mordermi remarked. "You'll want to choose your own from those we have, so I'll take you to our storeroom. My men and I steal only the very finest for ourselves."

"I'll pay you for all this when I can," Conan remembered.

"Pay us?" Mordermi clapped his shoulder. "Conan, I told you it's all *stolen*. Besides, without your intercession this morning, my rescue attempt would have been in just past the nick of time.''

"We but distribute to the people the products of their own labor, wrongfully appropriated from them by an unjust economic structure . . .''

"Oh, shut up, Santiddio!" Mordermi groaned. "Conan isn't joining us to hear your prattle!''

"But you *are* joining us?" Santiddio asked him.

Conan shrugged. "I joined Rimanendo's army in good faith; his government betrayed me. I killed an overbearing bully in a fight he demanded; General Korst would have hanged me. I don't quite understand your fine talk and theories, Santiddio, but I owe a grudge against Rimanendo and his tools—and I owe Mordermi for a sword.''

IV. Steel and Dreamers

"He and his friends may argue and posture like scatter-brained fools, but Santiddio's ideas are basically sound ones," Mordermi commented.

Somewhat defensively, so Conan thought. He studied the blade with a critical eye. There were several broadswords in the storeroom that Mordermi had dubbed his arsenal; Santiddio and his sister had left them while Conan made his selection. This one had a blade of watered steel that claimed Conan's attention—such blades were uncommon in the west.

"The two of you strike me as unlikely comrades," Conan said, testing the sword's balance.

"Why not?" Mordermi laughed bitterly. "The Pit is a haven for frustrated dreamers—be their dreams of wealth and station, or of artistic and social ideals. Rimanendo rules over Zingara like a bloated vampire, growing fat on our blood while his nobles devise new schemes to steal our wealth and our freedom. In another realm Santiddio would be free to put forward his arguments in the public forum—there to be ridiculed as a fool, or honored as a champion of the common folk. In Kordava they hang those whose dreams tempt them to speak out against an oppressive tyrant, just as they hang those whose dreams tempt them to steal the riches that tyranny has denied them.''

''Then you are part of the 'people's army' of the White Rose?''

''With all respect to Santiddio's feelings, the White Rose is a debating society, not an army by any stretch. Santiddio's friends represent the greatest intellects of Zingara, or so they tell me. They can quote to you from the massed political and social wisdom of countless philosophers and thinkers, living or long dead, in any language—but half of them couldn't guess which end of a sword to grasp if you gave them three chances.''

''I like this one,'' Conan decided. It was a fine weapon—a straight, wide, single-edged blade, with basket hilt and a complex guard of loops and shells. The watering was extremely delicate, and the layers seemed of infinite number.

''That is a splendid broadsword, isn't it,'' Mordermi agreed. ''I'd be curious to know its history—the hilt isn't original, I'm certain. I'd consider carrying that one myself perhaps, but the hilt is a bit clumsy for my hand, and a rapier is a more versatile weapon than the broadsword, I find. It's a lighter, more nimble blade—gives you a long reach in fencing, with the edge for the slash and the point for the thrust. Tradition still demands the hand-and-a-half sword for duelling, but in time I predict you'll see the rapier supplant the bastard sword, and the slash give way to the thrust.''

''There's not enough stopping power to a thrust from one of those narrow blades,'' Conan disagreed. ''I've seen a drunken Æsir mercenary take a rapier thrust through the heart, then go on to cut his slayer in half and kill two of his friends, before he stumbled over a bench and died. Split a man's skull, and if he doesn't fall, walk around and see what he's leaning against. You can have your fine techniques and rapier thrusts. Give me a strong blade with a good edge, and I'll cut my way out of any scrap.''

"Of course," Mordermi's tone held just enough sarcasm that Conan didn't miss it this time. "Well, I'm sure you made a believer out of Captain Rinnova though, didn't you? Do you want to try it?"

Mordermi drew his sword.

"Just to be certain you like the balance," he grinned. "First blood?"

Although Conan disliked the sham bloodletting that civilized men considered well-bred virility, the proposal was innocent enough. Conan wished he could read the lambent moods that flickered behind the veil of Mordermi's eyes.

Mordermi guarded himself, waiting politely for Conan to initiate the play. Conan, feeling foolish, made an awkward thrust that Mordermi easily evaded. There was nothing awkward to Mordermi's riposte, and Conan caught the rapier point upon his guard at the final instant.

Angered, Conan flung aside Mordermi's blade, rotated his wrist for an upward slash in the same movement. At the last moment he realized the swordtip would inflict a crippling wound to his friend's brachial plexus; he turned the point just as it touched the armpit, and Mordermi shivered away in the split second that Conan's hesitation had given him.

The slash would have inflicted permanent injury; shaken, Conan reminded himself that this was only a game. Mordermi felt no such qualms; before Conan could recover, his blade slashed for the Cimmerian's face. Conan parried desperately, but Mordermi was faster. Their blades rang together, sprang away. Conan felt a tug alongside his jaw. Already his broadsword, following the instinctive movement of his swordarm, was again engaged with Mordermi's blade as the other sought to withdraw. The heavier blade caught the rapier near its hilt, snagged the elaborate guard, and the force of Conan's blow ripped the hilt from Mordermi's hand.

"Conan!"

Sandokazi's scream snapped him to awareness. His

41

broadsword was raised for a killing blow. Mordermi was spinning to reach for his rapier—seemingly suspended in midair.

Conan froze. The rapier struck the floor, bounded upward. Mordermi caught it up.

"You're bleeding," Mordermi said calmly.

Conan touched his jaw. There was warm wetness from the shallow cut there.

"What madness is this?" Sandokazi demanded. "I heard the clash of steel . . ."

"Sorry," Conan muttered sheepishly, looking at the blood on his fingers. "I'm not used to doing this for sport."

"I should have known better than to relax my guard," Mordermi said easily. "No matter. The exercise was instructive."

"Mitra, what were you two . . . ?"

"Conan wanted to try the balance of his broadsword, and I was curious to test the swordarm that mastered Rinnova," Mordermi told her. "Conan has a theory . . ."

"That was a slash you used," Conan protested, remembering.

"As I said, a rapier is a versatile weapon," Mordermi shrugged. "You should have seen this, 'Kazi. Conan wields that broadsword as if it were an extension of his arm and no heavier than his finger."

"And you call Santiddio scatterbrained!" Sandokazi shook her head. "I think I'll catch up with my brother and listen to him exchange verbal barbs with his rivals. No blood to clean up afterward."

"Oh, don't bet on that," Mordermi murmured, as she stalked away. "Even Santiddio and Avvinti must eventually exhaust their repartee."

"If I were this Avvinti, I wouldn't want Sandokazi behind my back if it came to swordplay," Conan mused. "She showed no remorse this morning when she rode over the trampled bodies on the Dancing Floor. That rescue must have cost the lives of as many bystanders as combatants.''

''None of the Esanti blood ever let very much stand in the way of what they desired. You know, it was her idea to create a diversion with burning haywagons.'' He examined the slash on Conan's jaw. ''I've cut myself worse shaving.''

''The Esanti blood?'' Conan queried, thinking Mordermi's tone was edged with disappointment.

''Yes, Santiddio and Sandokazi are of the Esanti line—very high born, didn't you know? But I forget you are new to Kordava. The Esantis were one of the finest houses of Zingara. All that's gone now, of course, and only the three of them remain.''

He added: ''You'll want a dagger as well. See if any you find here will suit you.''

Conan eagerly looked over the row of knives that Mordermi indicated, thinking that there were weapons and armor here to equip a small army, should Santiddio's comrades decide to back their words with steel. ''You say there are three of them left of their house. Does the one hold title, while Santiddio and Sandokazi live as outcasts?''

''There is no title, no estate any longer. Only Santiddio and his sisters—they're triplets, did you know that? They were little more than children when their father offended King Rimanendo. I'm still not sure whether it was because the count was withholding more than his share of the royal taxes he collected from his tenants—as Rimanendo charged—or because he refused to levy the full burden of Rimanendo's taxes upon his people—as Santiddio claims. Little matter. He was beheaded, his lands and wealth given over to another of Rimanendo's henchmen. I forget what happened to the rest of the household—it wasn't anything to dwell upon.

''But a triple birth is a rare thing; I know of none other

43

in our lifetime in Zingara. Three is a sacred number, and they were spared if for no better reason than the awe of the common folk; a plain soldier is slower to defile the handiwork of his gods than is the officer who commands him. Through sympathizers of their father, they lived. Santiddio and Sandokazi eventually found their way to the Pit, as have so many. Loyal friends kept them in enough money to eke out an existence; Sandokazi dances, Santiddio draws from a portion of the funds collected by the White Rose.''

Conan found a heavy-bladed kidney dagger to his liking. ''And the third one?''

''That's Destandasi. She . . . well, she fell in with a different crowd, so to speak. She too was sickened by the corrupt tyranny of Rimanendo's rule, but while Santiddio and Sandokazi turned their energies toward social reform, Destandasi turned her back upon modern society. She entered the mysteries of Jhebbal Sag. I believe she is priestess in a grove sacred to Jhebbal Sag, somewhere beyond the Black River. There has been little or no communication obviously over the years. A sorceress—particularly one of that ancient cult—has little concern with the social and political upheavals of the modern world, for all that her brother and sister have been swept up in its tide.''

''Destandasi,'' Conan wondered, fitting the dagger to his belt. ''She is the twin of Sandokazi?''

''And of Santiddio,'' laughed Mordermi. ''Very aloof is Destandasi.''

V. Night Visitors

At the first whisper of sound, Conan was fully awake. His eyes slitted in the darkness of his chamber, and his fist closed upon the hilt of his dagger.

Mordermi had given over to him one of the rooms of the mansion. Conan had made up a pallet amidst the bales and piles of plundered goods from whence he could watch the door. It was the soft *snick* of the well-oiled bolt that had awakened him after only a few hours of sleep.

Someone had quickly cracked open the door and slipped past, of that Conan was certain—even though the door was again closed, and the room in total darkness. Unable to see, the intruder was waiting to orient himself within the cluttered storeroom. Silently, Conan slid from beneath his blanket and crept toward the almost indiscernible sound of soft breathing.

As he stealthily closed with the unseen visitor, Conan suddenly relaxed his tense grip upon the kidney dagger. To his nostrils came the piquant fragrance of perfume and sweat. Conan swept out his arm and gathered in a startled female form.

Sandokazi gave an involuntary yelp of surprise, then subsided in his embrace. The quick brush of his arms made it plain to Conan that the woman carried no weapon.

"I might have gutted you," Conan reproached her.

"Mitra! Are you a cat that you can see in the dark?"

"I heard your breathing, smelled your perfume." Conan wondered that he had to explain the obvious. "I thought I'd locked that door."

"Anyone can pick these locks," Sandokazi replied in the same tone. "But then, who would steal from Mordermi?"

"Indeed."

Sandokazi wore only a thin shift. Conan, who wore rather less, was keenly aware of the warm body that pressed against his own bare flesh.

"I danced until very late tonight," Sandokazi told him. "The others are all drunk and snoring after celebrating Santiddio's escape."

Conan, who had left the festivities earlier that evening, was not slow to comprehend. Perhaps had he not lingered along the way to his quarters with his convivial bath attendant, Conan's response now would have been different. The Cimmerian acted according to his savage code of honor—a code not overly governed by temperance—and the voluptuous figure that embraced him in the darkness was as tempting as any succubus.

"I told you I wouldn't forget what you did for my brother," Sandokazi whispered, her fingers teasing.

"You are Mordermi's woman," Conan reminded her with an effort.

"Mordermi need not know. He has not been my first lover, nor will he be my last. I'm no austere maiden like my sainted sister."

"It doesn't matter," Conan protested, knowing that if matters went any further his passions would override his ethics. "Mordermi is my host and my friend. I'll not cuckold him in his own house."

"Such piety!" Sandokazi scoffed. "Who would have believed it in a barbarian mercenary! My touch tells me that

46

you're not one of those who will only ride another stallion. Surely you're not afraid of Mordermi?''

Anger thickened Conan's tone. ''No doubt it's strange to you that I have not become sufficiently civilized to roll in the hay with a friend's woman. In Cimmeria our customs are somewhat archaic.''

''Well then, this isn't Cimmeria, is it,'' Sandokazi teased. ''Surely now, a man of your class hasn't paused to propose marriage to every wench he's tumbled!''

''Not to a slut,'' Conan snarled. Anger was now overruling the lust he felt for her. ''But if I care for a woman, then I make her my woman, and I'd kill any man who tried to steal my woman. Mordermi feels the same, if I'm any judge of men. If I take you for my own, it would mean a fight. I'm not ready to kill a friend over any woman.''

''Oh, so!'' Sandokazi drew away, her own temper aroused now. ''Santiddio was right—you are an altruist. Well, my possessive Cimmerian! I wasn't offering to become your barbarian hutmate in some stinking mountain village—I was offering you a night's pleasure! I was curious to learn whether there was a man underneath all that pretty muscle! Instead, all I find is one great hulking fool!''

As Sandokazi haughtily slipped from his grasp and made for the door, Conan almost agreed with her pronouncement. He was not accustomed to thinking through his actions, and only the fact that betrayal of a friend was abhorrent to his every instinct prevented him from seizing her and throwing her willing flesh down against his pallet. Instead, he let her go to the door.

After the total darkness of Conan's chamber, the gloom of the corridor beyond made a bright bar of light as the door opened. Sandokazi's bare tread had been soundless, so that the man outside the door was outlined in the band of light. Although taken unawares, he recovered instantly, and the knife in his hand gleamed balefully as he stabbed downward.

No less startled herself, Sandokazi screamed piercingly. The intruder's arm wavered involuntarily—he hadn't expected a woman—and that hesitation was enough for Sandokazi to writhe under the blow. With a dancer's litheness, she rolled into the hallway—taking a shallow cut as the blade sliced the shoulder of her shift. She screamed again.

The assailant whirled, still discomfited by the unexpected turn of events—uncertain whether to silence her or to attack the man he thought to find asleep here. Conan, lunging out of the darkness, struck first. Seizing the man's knife arm, he drove the kidney dagger into the intruder's belly, tearing upward in a gutting stroke that sheared into breastbone. The man's bellow of pain melted into a dull groan, as he sank from Conan's grasp and spilled onto the floor.

Sandokazi stopped screaming, and looked at Conan with glowing eyes.

By now other cries of alarm resounded throughout the mansion. Men came running into the hallway, blades bright in the light of the torches they carried. Mordermi was among them. There was question in his face, as he and his men took in the tableau.

Sandokazi did not hesitate. "I was about to retire, when I saw someone slinking along the hallway. His manner was suspicious; I followed him, and when he paused before Conan's door, I knew him to be an assassin. I screamed a warning to Conan; the assassin struck at me, and then Conan grappled with the man and killed him."

She drew down the slashed shoulder of her shift, examined the cut there. It bled freely, but was little more than a scratch. Conan had better sense than to contradict her story.

"You should have summoned one of us." Mordermi accepted her words. "You might have been killed."

"Summoned whom? You were all passed out over your cups."

"Turn him over, and let's see who he was," Mordermi

directed. "What kind of security do I have that lets Korst's assassins swagger through my quarters at will!"

They rolled the corpse onto its back, shoved a torch close to the bloody face. Several of them swore.

"Mitra! It's Velio!" Mordermi growled. "I held Velio one of my most trusted lieutenants. So Rimanendo's gold has corrupted even those I thought were my close friends! Conan, I offered you shelter here, and nearly caused your death."

Conan remained silent. In his own mind he was uncertain whether this Velio was indeed a spy and assassin—or a loyal henchman who, having witnessed Sandokazi's dalliance, was only intent upon avenging his lord's honor.

VI. At the King's Masque

The smell of the sea was warmed by the vast rose gardens that surrounded the royal pavilion beyond the high walls that enclosed the pleasure palace upon the shoreward side. Away from the waterfront squalor of Kordava's harbor, the royal pavilion thrust out into the sea from a lofty headland just beyond the city walls. A thousand festive lanterns made multicolored daylight about the gardens, while the laughter and gaiety of the guests drowned out the restive murmur of the surf in the darkness beneath the promontory.

Less festive than furtive, Conan moved among the guests of King Rimanendo's birthday masque—thinking that to-night's was a mad piece of daring, even for Mordermi, who had contrived to forge a quantity of royal invitations.

The Cimmerian cut a fantastic figure amidst the assembled wealth and nobility, and Conan was acutely self-conscious. He wore the horned helmet, scale armor and fur cloak of a Vanir warrior—a race he neither resembled nor loved. Henna gave his black mane an auburn tint, while a silken mask covered his upper features. The disguise was Sandokazi's idea, as was the heavy war axe he carried—a two-handed weapon with broad blade and hammer head. Conan approved of this last; weapons, other than a gentleman's rapier and

51

dagger, were suspect at the king's revel, but this axe was only part of his costume.

"Who would expect a real barbarian to masquerade as a barbarian?" Sandokazi had argued, displaying a Zingaran's tendency to lump all the dissimilar northern barbarians into one catchall. Conan spoke Zamoran well enough to pose as a visiting official from that distant realm—thus excusing his accent to the snobbish and parochial Zingaran gentry, most of whom would be hardpressed to distinguish a Pict from a Kushite, a Stygian from a Turanian, should so slight a matter have cause to impinge upon their attention.

Sandokazi herself wore a falcon's mask, full-face, and an enveloping cape of feathers that swirled about her bare limbs as she walked. She wore nothing beneath the feathered cloak.

Santiddio, who led her about upon a silver chain affixed to her neck, wore a falconer's garb and a domino mask. As Sandokazi had predicted, none of the guests paid him a second glance.

Strangest of all, Mordermi capered about in an idealized guise of King Rimanendo himself—in ermine robes, gilt mail, tinsel crown, powdered hair, sufficient belly padding to alter his own physique without blaspheming that of Zingara's monarch. Again, Sandokazi's idea; "Will they look askant upon the image of our king?"

She was, to Conan's mind, exceedingly clever, and he was just as relieved that there had been no further nocturnal visits during the month he had remained with Mordermi.

The weeks had passed quickly and not unprofitably for Conan. The pickings were rich for Mordermi and his band, and Mordermi was a generous leader. Conan himself was no slouch when it came to the unlawful acquisition of property, and the Cimmerian gave away nothing in daring or ability to the more experienced Zingaran rogue. Admiration grew into a firm friendship between the two, tempered with an undercurrent of rivalry which, in their youth, neither man yet recognized as a threat.

It was a friendship that included Santiddio and Sandokazi, although there was never the kinship of spirit that made a bond between Conan and Mordermi. Mordermi was a barbarian of the urban slums in effect, forged in a wilderness as savage and pitiless in its way as the cold mountains of Cimmeria. With Santiddio and Sandokazi there was always that aloof barrier engendered by higher breeding. For all his talk of the brotherhood of all mankind, Santiddio's intellectuality effectively divorced him from the realities of his dreams, while there was to Sandokazi the sense of an amused participant in a game that seems somehow too childish for one of her accomplishments.

Conan sensed that he himself was as much of an enigma to the others, and that perhaps their friendship was nourished by the fact that they were all of them misfits: Mordermi whose ambitions were far more subtle than merely to reign as prince of thieves. Sandokazi, whose amusement was to pull down the social order that was her birthright. Santiddio, whose dream was to create a new order based upon reason, not power. And finally Conan, a barbarian adventurer who had left Cimmeria to see the civilized kingdoms of mankind, and had found little to vindicate his wanderlust.

He had sought adventure, and in that Conan had never been disappointed.

There were several hundred guests here to celebrate King Rimanendo's birthday masque. Fantastically costumed figures promenaded about the garden and grounds, while within the pavilion courtly gentlemen and their gorgeously gowned ladies swirled in dance upon the black marble floor. Scantily clad serving girls darted about with golden trays of sweetmeats and choice delicacies, brimming silver goblets of rare wines and iced punches. Amorous couples dwindled into the privacy of arbors and floral-scented bowers, where the

53

laughter and music of the masque muffled their silken rustlings and soft sighs.

Conan ate sparingly, but tossed down whatever goblet was offered him, quaffing century-old vintages as if they were cheap ale. To those guests who accosted him, Conan grunted curt replies in Zamoran. Of menacing aspect, the royal guests judged him drunk and boorish. Conan was not drunk.

This night's adventure was not to his liking, although Mordermi saw it as a splendid jest. Conan preferred more stealthy theft, or else open brigandry—break into a wealthy lord's treasure vault, or sack a merchant's caravan. Mordermi's scheme tonight ran the risks of both methods. As such, Conan was not overconcerned; the elaborate charade did annoy him.

Besides themselves, Mordermi had contrived to place another score of his men and as many of the White Rose within the royal pleasure palace. Most were in the guise of servants and lackeys, although a number of Santiddio's associates were of sufficient presence to masquerade as guests. Weapons were the crucial point; one does not come heavily armed to honor his king's birthday. Of course, no gentleman would appear at a court festival without his rapier, while his lackey would be expected to carry a knife or bludgeon against thieves and footpads. Conan, Mordermi pointed out when the Cimmerian wanted to lead the outside assault, must serve as a one-man shock troop for those within the walled gardens.

The royal pleasure palace—bordered by high walls and sea-torn cliffs, guarded by Rimanendo's personal troops. The scheme—daring beyond belief. The risks—bordering on the suicidal. The prize—the gold and jewels of Zingara's wealthiest aristocracy.

A red-haired girl, wearing only a scanty halter and G-string fashioned of interlinked silver discs and dragging a two-handed sword in an absurd portrayal of a barbarian swordswoman, tilted her smiling face toward Conan's scowl. "Why so sombre, my fellow barbarian?" she trilled. "I know a quiet spot where we two can repair to wage a friendly struggle. After all, it is not yet the time for removing our . . . masks."

"Is it not yet midnight?" Conan asked in a thick accent. "But it is almost time for the pretty falcon to dance, as she has promised."

The girl made a face behind her mask. "If you want to *watch* some fool dance, don't let me detain you."

"Bitch!" Conan mumbled, as she clanked away. His temper was not the sweeter for all the wine he had drunk. On his own, he would have taken the highborn tart on her offer, turned her playful scorn into a different mood, then gone on about his larcenous endeavours. But this was Mordermi's game, and Conan must play his part—or the carefully planned raid would turn into a death-trap for all of them.

Conan sourly let a serving wench refill his goblet, then strode off toward the pavilion where Sandokazi was to begin her dance. The prospect of imminent fighting soothed the Cimmerian's temper—where another man would instead have grown raw-nerved from the tension.

That one of the royal guests might desire to dance before the others like an entertainer in some low tavern was not strange—for this was the king's birthday masque, when Zingara's aristocracy might shed their courtly dignity and act out the whims and passions that lurked behind the masks of their well-bred hauteur. Chaste matrons might cavort about as painted hoydens; austere lords might mince upon the dance floor in the seductive gowns of a demimonde; maidenly daughters might flaunt their white flesh in the scantiest of costumes before the hot eyes of young gentlemen whose fanciful attire revealed rather than concealed their virile curves.

Presiding over his birthday revel, King Rimanendo smiled down from his royal box upon the guests who caroused upon the black marble floor beneath the gallery. His Majesty had already drunk more than was his wont for the occasion, and the smile upon his loose-featured face was more vacuous than usual. His corpulent figure seemed to be poured half in, half out of his velvet-padded chair of state. A young boy, whose naked flesh glowed with scented oils, held a chalice of opiated wine to his master's lips on command, while his twin daintily wiped the trickles of wine and sweat from the rolls of chin.

A number of Rimanendo's choice circle of sycophants and courtiers shared the royal box, while the remainder of the gallery was filled for the most part by vigilant soldiers of the king's personal guard. King Rimanendo was not yet fool enough to forget that many of his guests here tonight would carouse all the more abandonedly at his royal wake.

Sandokazi's appearance had excited comment even amidst the naked debauchery of this night's revel. Bare flesh was cheap tonight—its lure derived from a society in which a wellborn lady customarily wore enough clothing from ankle to neck to require two attendants to help her dress. While girls of high rank brazenly paraded their barely costumed bodies, Sandokazi lured and tempted with too-brief glimpses of her supple dancer's figure beneath the fluttering streamers of her feathered cloak. When she had promised to dance for them in the hour before unmasking, excitement grew high as that hour approached.

They made way for her within the pavilion, clearing a space upon the polished marble floor. Sandokazi spoke briefly with the musicians—she had made arrangements with them earlier in the evening—and they began to ply their strings and flutes and drums in a quick, trilling melody. Conan knew too little about music to recognize the piece, but the rest of the growing audience made a bright chatter of applause.

She stood for a moment in the center of the circle they had cleared for her—a fantastic figure even beside those who gathered to watch her dance. Her feathered cape completely enveloped her from neck to ankles as she paused there motionlessly. Behind the falcon mask that entirely enclosed her head, her glowing eyes stared back at them without blinking. Then Santiddio unfastened the silver chain from the collar at his sister's throat, and stepped away.

Freed from this tether, Sandokazi leaped from the polished floor in a sudden great bound, throwing her arms outward in a gesture that raised her cloak from her side like the spreading wings of a bird taking flight. For a moment Sandokazi seemed to hang suspended in midair, her lithe figure completely naked as her feathered wings bore her on high. Then, even as breath caught in hundreds of throats, she had fallen lightly to the marble floor, her nudity concealed once more by the flurry of feathers.

Across the black marble floor Sandokazi danced now—sweeping low, spinning gracefully, then rising into the air in a sudden leap. So swift were her movements that the wreaths of white and umber feathers swirled all about her like living wings—one instant revealing a blur of white breast or tanned thigh, in another heartbeat molding close to her figure in a second skin. The musicians increased the tempo of their shrill melody, and Sandokazi seemed to fly about the ebon floor—soaring, darting, rising, diving. Her audience, remembering that first leaping vision of naked beauty, watched entrancedly as the flurry of her cloak enticed their eyes with the instantaneous disclosing and veiling of the dancer's charms.

Faster and faster the tempo of her flight. Only a trained danseuse could have maintained such a pace, mastered the intricate gestures and movements. Many of the watchers speculated as to whose face might be hidden beneath the falcon mask, enraptured by the beauty that was not concealed to them.

At last, as the frenetic music reached a crescendo, Sandokazi once again leapt high into the air, arms outspread, pirouetting in midair. Her cloak of feathers spun straight out from her shoulders, disclosing her entire figure in nude perfection, as she seemed to take flight above the polished floor. Trailing her wings, she dropped back to the marble— as lightly as a falcon returning to its perch. Gathering her cape about her, Sandokazi made a low bow to her entranced audience.

"My lords and my ladies!" shouted Santiddio, rejoining his sister through the tumultuous applause. "You have seen the dance of the falcon! But recall that the falcon is a bird of prey—for now you must pay the price of your entertainment!"

At first they thought he only meant for them to shower her with coins and trinkets, as they might a common dancer. But angry shouts and cries of alarm quickly disabused them.

"Softly, my lords!" Santiddio warned, drawing his rapier. "It's only your gold and jewels we want, not your lives!"

Milling in sudden confusion, the assembled guests seemed unable to grasp that this was not all some elaborate jest. While they had been intent upon Sandokazi's dance, Mordermi's men had stealthily taken position at the doorways. Now all entrances to the pavilion were barred by grim-faced brigands with naked weapons in their fists. In the gardens without, frightened revellers fled from the threatening figures who suddenly sprang out of the darkness beyond the multicolored lanterns.

"Stand where you are, all of you!" Mordermi shouted, leaping onto a table and brandishing his sword. "A hundred of my men have surrounded the pavilion! Make no resistance, and you'll not be harmed!''

A few men, out of rashness born of disbelief or drunkenness, sought to draw their weapons. In an instant Mordermi's men were upon them, bludgeons and swords striking savagely. Women screamed in horror, as bright blood and groans of agony punctuated the quick fate of futile resistance. The king's guests had come to the masque to disport; Mordermi's brigands had come to despoil. The outlaws were armed and organized, and their surprise attack left no time for the guests to rally. Those of the men who wore arms were speedily divested of their weapons—either passively or by force—and their swords distributed to those of the attackers who might need them. In a moment, panic claimed the guests—so that they milled helplessly about the ballroom.

At the first ripple of drawn steel and violent bloodshed, King Rimanendo's guard instinctively made for the dance floor. The move was expected. Conan, uttering a satisfied belch, took a good grip on the haft of his war axe and positioned himself at the stairway leading down from the gallery. Several of his cohorts rushed to join him there, carrying chairs and tables for a barricade.

"Stand clear, and give me room to swing!" Conan roared. "I can hold the stairway against a thousand of these perfumed toy soldiers! Come down to me, you glittering fops! Who'll die first!"

Conan's boast might well have been true. Only a few men could descend the steep stairway at a time. The royal guard were resplendent in silks and velvet and silvered mail, but their halbards were unwieldy on the narrow stairway, and they had no archers among them who might pick off the raiders as the guardsmen advanced.

"Come back to me, you fools!" Rimanendo shrilled, as his besotted brain recognized danger. "Close about me, do you hear! They seek to murder your king! I'll have flayed alive any man of you who deserts me!''

The king of Zingara hugged his catamites to his quaking breast. Bleating in fear, he begged his soldiers to surround him, to fight to the last drop of their blood to defend him from this army of assassins. ''Let those on the floor escape as best they can!'' he commanded. ''Mitra, how they're screaming! Why haven't my soldiers at the gate come to save their king from his murderers!''

A strong garrison was positioned along the gate and high wall that shut off the royal pleasure palace from the mainland, while other guards regularly patrolled the crest of the steep cliffs that bounded the promontory as it thrust seaward. Their presence was primarily to insure the privacy of the king and his party and to discourage thieves, rather than to repel an armed assault—Zingara was not at war, despite the internal dissensions and rivalries that gave assassins certain employ.

As Sandokazi's dance had reached its climax, Mordermi had signed to one of his men outside the pavilion. The man in turn had passed the signal to those who lay hidden beyond the walls.

From the darkened trees that lined the road that led to the king's pleasure gardens, torches suddenly flared to brightness. Angry shouts filled the night, as a disordered mob suddenly converged upon the gate. A hundred or more members of the White Rose—as close to a muster of Santiddio's vaunted people's army as had ever been attempted—stormed out of the night in an unruly procession, brandishing placards and chanting slogans.

''Disperse!'' commanded the captain of the guard. ''Disperse at once! Do you hear!'' He sent a frantic summons for the rest of his soldiers to reinforce his guards here at the gate.

''We'll not disperse until we've had an audience with

King Rimanendo!'' yelled back their burly leader. It was Carico, most radical of Santiddio's rivals for leadership of the White Rose, who exulted in the prestige this night's work would surely bring to him. ''Our king and his effete nobility pass the night in drunken debauchery, while in Kordava widows and children must dine on refuse and sleep in gutters!''

''Disperse, or I'll send out my soldiers to crack a few heads!''

''We'll not disperse without an audience with Rimanendo!'' Carico roared above the jeers of his comrades. ''The people are starving, while the tyrant and his henchmen feast upon the blood of our land!''

''Call out the archers!'' ordered the worried captain to a subordinate, as a hail of stone and refuse began to pelt the gate. ''If this disturbance reaches the attention of His Majesty, he'll have my head!''

Thus, even as the applause rose for Sandokazi's dance, the soldiers who should have been posted about the wall and grounds were racing toward the melee outside the main gate. In the distance, the tumult beyond the wall did not reach the ears of those within the pavilion—no more than the soldiers who faced the angry mob at the gate were yet aware of the sudden uproar that was bringing a violent climax to the birthday revel.

In a short time screams from the pavilion, frightened fugitives who had been at dalliance in the gardens outside would alert the soldiers at the gate to the real danger. Before they could recover, Mordermi and his band must be in flight. Holding sway over a ballroom full of drunken revellers and fainting women was an easier task than facing down a force of heavily armed soldiers.

While Rimanendo cowered behind the protective wall of his personal guard, Mordermi's brigands rapidly despoiled the royal guests of their valuables—working with systematic skill for all the need of haste. This had been a major court festival; lords and their ladies alike had come adorned in their most magnificent jewellery. Now costly rings, necklaces and tiaras of incalculable value, jeweled daggers and almoners bulging with gold and silver coins were stripped unceremoniously from the terrified guests, stuffed into sturdy sacks. Others quickly collected silver plates and chalices, golden trays and candelabra.

Sandokazi, laughing excitedly behind her mask, scurried about with an open sack—speedily filling it with a fortune in gold and jewellery, while her brother stood at her side with drawn rapier. After the initial ripple of violence, there had been little resistance to the raiders. Women whimpered as they surrendered their precious ornaments, while men scowled and muttered low threats of vengeance. But half a dozen crumpled figures on the polished floor and a number more who nursed broken scalps and bleeding wounds were evidence that the outlaws were not overawed by their victims' lofty status.

Conan shook a cramp from his tense shoulders and glowered uneasily at the guards atop the stairway. There would be hard fighting should they determine to descend from the gallery. The Cimmerian wondered that these Zingarans could honor as their king a drunken coward who permitted his nobles to be plundered before his presence and refused to allow his soldiers to interfere.

"Quickly now, my loyal subjects!" urged Mordermi, clapping his hands and prancing all about. In his guise of King Rimanendo, the travesty became unbearable, although the humor of it was little appreciated by His Majesty's court.

The looting of the royal pavilion proceeded swiftly. In a matter of minutes the raiders were weighted down with as many overladen sacks as they might feasibly make off with. Mordermi judged that it was time to bid his host a good night and depart—before reinforcements ruined the evening for them.

"You will all remain inside, if you care to live through this night!" Mordermi warned in a loud voice. "I have archers positioned outside the doorways. Any fool who tries to pursue us from here will be given a wooden stickpin to wear upon his heart!"

Wondering how long that bluff would hold them, Conan warily followed his comrades from the pavilion. If the Zingaran gentry were made of the same stuff as their king, he decided, then they would probably remain inside until they starved.

They had little more than fled the pavilion, when shouts and the clamour of running soldiers told them how closely they had timed it.

Faced with the threat of archers, the mob at the gate had broken for cover. From the shelter of the darkened trees, they had continued to hurl stones and verbal abuse at the guards—Carico haranguing them at the top of his stout lungs. Flames crackled upward from the midst of the road, and a grotesque effigy of King Rimanendo began to burn lustily.

Enraged, the captain of the guard had ordered his archers to loose upon the rabble. A few howls of pain rewarded their efforts, but the archers were few and their targets hidden by the night and the forest. Reasonably protected from the desultory archery barrage, the mob seemed more incensed than cowed by the show of force, and the riot before the royal pleasure gardens only waxed the more furious.

Not waiting for new troops to reach them from the city, the captain of the guard had ordered a sortie to break up the rioters. A strong detachment of his force had just marched out of the gate, when word of the raid upon the king's pavilion reached him. In an agony of indecision, the officer sought to call back his sally to defend the gate once again, so that he could dispatch another body of troops to the pavilion—all the while uncertain which of these threats constituted the main attacking force.

As a result, it was a disordered and winded party of guards who reached the plundered pavilion too late to trap Mordermi's raiders within the marble structure. Instead, they came upon a frightened and outraged mass of royal guests, bereft of their valuables and angrily demanding the heads of all those concerned—incompetent guards included.

With a scant lead, Mordermi and his treasure-laden band raced through the darkened grounds beyond the lighted gardens. While they were ahead of the chase for the moment, they had not made good their escape by any means. Sheer cliffs dropped away into the sea on all sides of the headland beyond its walled landward side—and there was no chance of scaling the wall now that the garrison was fully alerted.

The third phase of Mordermi's raid must work perfectly now, or they would be hunted down like wolves trapped in a sheep pen.

Out of the mist-buried sea, a small flotilla of rowboats fought the tide to gain a narrow fringe of beach exposed as the sea ebbed from beneath the sheer bluff. With precise timing, they breached the surf and touched shore in the interval that the guards who should have patrolled the cliffs were decoyed to repel the rioters at the gate. Previous reconnaissance had settled upon the best approach to the headland, and now the hotly pursued raiders made for the prearranged landing site.

The promontory rose a hundred feet or more above the surf—its escarpment a sheer wall of broken rock. As they reached the pick-up point, one of those on the beach below shot an arrow to which a cord was affixed. Eager hands hauled in the cord, after its nether end had been made fast to a heavy rope. Drawing the rope upward, they secured it to a tree that was firmly rooted close beside the precipice.

Clinging to the rope, the raiders hurriedly worked their way down the face of the cliff—their descent encumbered by their weighty sacks of plunder.

Conan tore off the silken mask that covered his features and glared back along the path they had followed. The grounds were extensive, and along the edge of the cliffs stunted trees replaced roses and floral arbors. With the cover of darkness, it was impossible to know which way the outlaws had fled, and this had given them a distinct advantage over their pursuers. But Conan could hear the frantic sounds of men crashing through the brush, fanning out in their search, and he knew that time was running out for them.

"Get on down there, 'Kazi!" Mordermi urged her. "We may have fighting here very shortly."

"I'll wait for the rest of you," Sandokazi returned.

"Santiddio, see that your sister gets down that rope, or I'll toss her off and let the falcon fly home. Conan and I will guard the rear."

Conan observed the progress of the others down the rope. "We'd all be down in no time, if they'd just let those sacks drop and slide down after them."

"What! And risk losing all these lovely baubles in the surf?" Mordermi demanded incredulously. "Conan, what's the point in stealing all this gold if we don't mean to spend it?"

"Look sharp, then," Conan warned. "Here comes some who don't mean to let us live to spend it!"

The first straggling group of soldiers pelted toward them, howling like a pack with its quarry at bay. The light was just enough for them to discern the raiders silhouetted along the edge of the precipice, so that they shouted to their comrades that the outlaws were trapped.

Conan risked a glance toward the rope. Most of the men had made it down; others were scrambling in mad haste. But they would have to deal with these soldiers before he and Mordermi could make good their escape.

The soldiers were breathless from the pursuit, but they were ready enough with their swords. Conan, in helmet and scale armor, had the advantage over his comrades, and he unhesitatingly attacked the first of the guard to reach them. Swinging the war axe with both hands, Conan's heavy blade snapped the other's rapier as it made a futile parry, sheared through cuirass and caved in the man's chest. Wrenching the axe free, Conan parried another's blade against the iron straps that reinforced its haft, smashed the man's arm with a sudden blow of the hammer head, then finished him with a slash of the broad blade.

Beside him, Mordermi was engaged with another of the kings's soldiers. Clearly the superior swordsman, Mordermi was held in check momentarily by the guard's cuirass. Lunging swiftly, he evaded his opponent's attempt to parry, and thrust his rapier tip through the unprotected throat above the cuirass. Giving back as another guardsman rushed past the toppling body, Mordermi stumbled—as a third assailant dropped low and ripped his blade through the outlaw's belly in a disembowelling stroke.

Conan spun from his own dying opponent, to split the man's skull as he straightened from dealing Mordermi his mortal wound. To the Cimmerian's astonishment, Mordermi only laughed and ran his blade through the thigh of his other assailant, killing him as he crumpled from the blow. Not blood and entrails, but great clods of padding were spilling from the bandit chieftain's belly—the blade had only slashed through his burlesque guise of Rimanendo.

"Get down the rope, before more of them come!" Conan shouted.

"I'll stand rearguard," Mordermi told him. "Get going yourself."

Conan's retort was cut short, as Mordermi suddenly grunted and staggered backward from the edge of the cliff.

His eyes widened in disbelief at the arrow that sprouted from his left shoulder.

Conan flung himself down, as a second shaft hissed past him. Cursing, Mordermi dropped beside him. Near by, they could hear the main force of the guards closing in on them. Another arrow shattered against a rock beside their heads.

"Is it bad?" Conan asked, trying to look past Mordermi's bloody fingers that clutched his wound.

"It missed my heart, if that's what you mean," Mordermi hissed through gritted teeth. "But it seems I must climb down the rope one-handed. Get going, will you! I'll follow as fast as I can!"

"Crom! You're a stubborn ass!" Conan swore. He was watching the line of trees behind them. Mordermi saw nothing, but as the next arrow stabbed into the earth beside them, Conan leaped up and hurled the heavy axe. A scream of death agony burst out for an instant and choked off.

"Only the one archer, I think," Conan judged, hauling at Mordermi. "Quick, before the others catch up to us! We'll take it together."

In desperate haste, they dropped over the lip of the escarpment—Conan going first so that he might support Mordermi's weight. It was awkward, but they managed to make scrambling progress—descending by pushing out from the near vertical face of broken rock with their feet and braking their slide by hanging to the rope.

They had almost reached the shoreline below, when the rope jerked spasmodically, then went slack. Mordermi clawed out as they started to fall—the beach was thirty feet or more below them, and rocks awaited their flesh.

Then Conan crushed the smaller man in against the face of the bluff. Clinging with one hand to a crack in the escarpment, Conan held Mordermi tightly in his other arm. The severed length of rope spilled past them in aimless coils. From below they heard cries of consternation.

"I felt the rope shiver as they hacked it apart," Conan said. "The cliff is broken up enough here so that I found a handhold in time."

"We're trapped," Mordermi cursed. "There's no way down without a rope."

Conan snorted. "In Cimmeria babes learn to scale mountain precipices before they can walk on flat ground. This is a garden path. Hang on to me, if you won't climb down yourself."

All but helpless, Mordermi clung to Conan and tried to support his dead weight as best he could with his crippled left arm. The cliff seemed sheer as a pane of glass, its face hidden by sea-mist that drowned even the starlight. The rocks were slick with spray from the surf below, and a slippery coating of moss and seaweed made their descent the more perilous with each foot they crawled.

Yet Conan clambered down the escarpment with the ease of an ape climbing out of a tree, seemingly heedless of Mordermi's clinging weight. It was an interval that Mordermi would never forget, although it could not have been much more than a minute or so before Conan dropped the remaining distance to safety on the beach below.

"Did you decide to take a short cut?" Santiddio laughed uneasily. "We saw the rope come down, and wondered what was coming after."

"Half of Rimanendo's army, if we wait long enough," Conan growled. "Mordermi's already caught an arrow, and there'll be more any second."

"Cast off! Why are you waiting?" Mordermi yelled, his face ashen from lost blood. "Conan, I'll not forget this."

"You saved me from the gallows," Conan told him as they waded into the surf to cast off. "I always pay my debts."

VII. Golden Light, Blue Light

Mordermi's face bore an unnatural pallor, but there was nothing of infirmity in his smile as he held a lustrous necklace of matched pearls to the golden candlelight.

"Sandokazi, this is yours. Count it as having come out of my share. None of us could have danced well enough to gull those sheep into lining up so conveniently for the shearing."

Mordermi's left shoulder was rebandaged, and he was still bare above the waist. They had cut the arrow out of his flesh before that dawn, after returning to the Pit without incident through one of the tunnels that connected the underground warren with the waterfront. The arrow had been deflected by bone, had lodged in the thick muscle of Mordermi's shoulder — inflicting no grievous hurt once the bleeding was stopped. Sleep had restored much of his strength, and the prospect of the raid's fantastic plunder further revitalized him.

They sat at ease within Mordermi's headquarters: Conan, breaking his fast over a rind of cheese and loaf of coarse break; Santiddio, dishevelled and sleepless from excitement; Sandokazi, smiling as she tried the pearls about her throat; Mordermi, eyes aglow as he contemplated the results of a theft that would make his name a legend within the brotherhood of thieves.

In the center of the panelled chamber, a massive mahogany banquet table sagged under the weight of the gold and silver that was stacked upon its boards. The sheer mass of the jewellery alone represented a fortune beyond their powers to comprehend. A sidereal moraine of rings and necklaces, pendants and tiaras, earrings and brooches—it was as if all the stars in the firmament had been heaped upon the table. Beside this dazzling mound of precious stones, the sprawling mountains of gold and silver plate seemed tawdry and insignificant.

"Do you know?" Mordermi sighed contentedly. "Dividing all of this into shares is going to be a more difficult task than was the stealing of it."

"But a more pleasant one, I think," Santiddio purred.

Conan washed down a mouthful of dark bread with a swallow of wine from a golden chalice. "You may find the task is no less dangerous. These baubles are pretty to look at, but I'd prefer a chest of coins any day. We can't just open up a stall on market day and sell this stuff off to whoever walks by."

"No problem," Mordermi assured him easily. "We'll handle this as if it were any ordinary theft. I have the organization, after all. We'll melt down the gold and silver plate into bullion—that can't be traced—and dispose of the jewels through my connections in Aquilonia. Even with a cut here and a cut there, there's enough wealth here to buy all of Zingara and hire Rimanendo to clean sponges in the public baths."

"It's too much money," Conan persisted. "That's the danger." He sipped his wine and declined to express himself further.

"And half of it goes to the White Rose," Santiddio

exulted, ignoring Conan's misgivings—the Cimmerian was ever a man of sombre mood.

"And well earned," Mordermi agreed. "I'll confess now that I had my doubts as to whether your people could carry out their end of things."

"I, too, have my organization," Santiddio told him smugly.

"That will be your organization now," Sandokazi said sarcastically, as there came a knocking at the chamber door.

One of Mordermi's men—the bandit's headquarters was like an armed camp following the raid—opened the door to admit Avvinti and Carico. Their arrival was so punctual that they could only have come early and waited without until the appointed time. Avvinti bowed with precise formality as he entered; Carico shouted a boisterous greeting and shook hands. The faces of both men registered awe at the sight of the plunder.

The two men—Santiddio's chief rivals for leadership of the White Rose—were not friends for all of Santiddio's rhetoric of a common cause. Avvinti, tall and poised, physically resembled Santiddio with his aristocratic features and wellborn manner. The fourth son of a noble house and excessively educated, his likeness to Santiddio was a source of jealousy rather than a common bond. Conan despised him. Carico was of a different mold—uncouth, sweaty, coarse-featured and barrel-chested. He had the massive shoulders and sooty complexion of a blacksmith, which trade he pursued—when not breaking up the secret meetings of the White Rose by propounding some new bit of radical thought. For although without formal education, Carico was a great thinker—a quality his followers extolled. Conan, whose father had been a blacksmith, thought Carico a good drinking companion and better at arm-wrestling than speechmaking.

Santiddio's politics fell somewhere in between Avvinti's doctrine of benevolent dictatorship through an intellectual elite and Carico's classless utopia that would be achieved through an alliance of agrarian peasant and urban laborer. As such, while both factions denounced him, he drew majority support from those who were alienated by either extreme. As a consequence, it was Santiddio's leadership that held the White Rose together.

"Impressive, isn't it?" remarked Santiddio, as the two newcomers continued to gape speechlessly.

"There's gold enough here to feed all of Zingara's poor for a year!" Carico exclaimed.

"Enough for the White Rose to establish the organizational power base that we must have," Avvinti said sententiously, "if our movement is to emerge as a force to be reckoned with in Zingaran politics."

"We can discuss how our share of the loot is to be distributed at our next meeting," Santiddio interrupted their nascent quarrel. "Mordermi will need time to fence all of this discreetly."

"How much time?" demanded Avvinti suspiciously.

"All that depends on General Korst," Mordermi snapped back at him. "We'll move as quickly as we dare—only a fool would risk getting caught with loot that can be identified so readily. I'm counting on the fact that our escape by sea will lead him to concentrate his first efforts against ships lying off the harbor. But this is no ordinary theft, and Korst knows that his position hangs on placating Rimanendo's wrath. We must use extreme caution."

"Why not divide up just the coins now, then?" Carico suggested. "We both have immediate expenses to satisfy, after all. I for one fully trust Mordermi to fence the rest of this treasure as fairly and as speedily as possible."

"I'll go with that, of course," Santiddio seconded. "Avvinti?"

"We could divide the entire mass of gold and jewels right now," Avvinti argued. "I'm sure we could dispose of our half of the loot through the White Rose—just as efficiently and with less chance of being cheated."

Mordermi smiled thinly. "Cheated?" Cold light flickered behind his veiled eyes. His swordarm was uninjured, and his hand rested negligently upon his rapier hilt.

"By middlemen," Avvinti hastily explained.

"How many fences do you know?" Carico wondered caustically.

"And we will need an expert's eye to appraise this hoard," Santiddio sneered. "Shall we permit a Shemite jewel merchant to give us full value for each piece, or shall we just hack every ring and necklace into halves?"

"I only want whatever is best for the White Rose," Avvinti said coldly. "You'll forgive me if I may have had less experience than some in matters relating to the dispersal of stolen property."

Conan, who had seen this sort of dispute arise too often before, remained silent. Mordermi did not miss the fact that Conan ate with only his left hand, while his right hand hung close to the hilt of his broadsword.

Avvinti was not so obtuse as to fail to realize how matters stood. "If this is the will of the majority, then of course I must agree," he conceded with ill grace. "Shall we get on with dividing just the money, then?"

"Good," Mordermi concluded. "Then we'll count out the coins into two shares. I have scales, if you wish—or shall we just assume that our worthy masters wouldn't stoop to give us fraudulent coinage?"

The mood lightened in that moment of anticipation, as Sandokazi leaned across the table to drag the heavy purses of gold and silver and copper coins toward Mordermi. Faces leaned forward intently, as the bright glitter of coinage spilled a trail across the stained mahogany boards.

73

They were so intent, that only Conan noticed that the candle flames suddenly burned with a blue nimbus. The Cimmerian rubbed his eyes. The yellow flames seemed to dwindle beneath a veil of blue. Conan started to speak.

The door opened. Suddenly, silently, without announcement. Touched by the bluish glow of the candles, a stranger stood upon the threshold. Unbidden, he entered their chamber. The door swung shut of its own, but not before Conan saw the motionless figures of Mordermi's men standing indifferently at their posts.

It happened so suddenly, so unexpectedly, that time seemed to hang suspended before anyone moved.

Mordermi was the first to speak "Who are you—and how did you get in here?"

"My name is Callidios," the newcomer replied in a tone of irony. "I walked in here."

"I'd left orders not to be disturbed," Mordermi growled, angered over the interruption and the breach of security.

"No one told me," the stranger rejoined.

"Well then, why are you here?"

"I've come to make you a king."

Conan's fist closed about his swordhilt, but Mordermi only laughed—as did the others after a nervous pause. This calm assertion, uttered within this den of rogues and killers, was surely a pointless jest. But Conan did not join in their laughter, for he felt the chill breath of sorcery in this, and the stranger's accent was of Stygia.

Callidios was not a presence to radiate menace. He was young—apparently no older than any of those here—and his figure was thin and loose-limbed beneath doublet and trunk hose that wanted mending. A loose cloak of gray stuff was slung haphazardly about his narrow shoulders, and he slouched crookedly from one hip to the other, so that he seemed about to trip over the long rapier he wore too low from his hips. He had the dusky complexion and hawk-nosed features of a high caste Stygian, but the lank straw-colored hair and gray-green eyes evidenced his mongrel bloodline. Between the limp hair and shadowed eyes was an impressive expanse of brow, although the aura of great intellect was marred by the thin lips that twitched aimlessly and the too-lustrous eyes that hinted of lotus dreams.

"Once more, before my men come to crack a few ribs, what are you doing here?"

"Call your men, but you'll hear no answer," Callidios smiled, shifting weight to his other hip. "They sleep too soundly. Perhaps they kept late hours last night."

"Sifino! Amosi!" Mordermi shouted. "Come and knock this damn fool loose from his teeth!"

When there came no response, Mordermi repeated his demands, somewhat more luridly, but with no better result.

"It is a simple spell," Callidios shrugged. "I know at least one other. Don't draw your swords, gentlemen! If I intended mischief, you'd have known of it before now."

"Conan, kill this bloody fool if he makes one more move," Mordermi snarled. "Santiddio, see what's going on outside in the hallway."

Santiddio started to obey, then froze. There was no longer a door to the chamber. Only a blank wall where the doorway had stood.

"A childish illusion, I'll admit," Callidios apologized. "It may be that the doorway is still there, I'm really not sure. But forgive my precautions. This council should not reach any beyond our small circle."

Callidios made no discernible movement, but suddenly the doorway had reappeared. From the hallway beyond, they could hear dim voices shouting accusations.

"It was nothing very imaginative," Callidios shrugged.

"Wait, Conan!" Mordermi forestalled the Cimmerian's murderous lunge. "Let's hear him out. Our visitor is a man of subtle talents."

"He's a Stygian sorcerer, and he'll seem less subtle when he's shorter by a head," Conan spat. "Kill him now, or we'll all live to regret it."

"In a moment, perhaps," Mordermi suggested, as the others seemed to be of Conan's mind. "But since Callidios has sought out our council, let's allow him to explain his presence here."

"Easily done," Callidios said languidly. "I've come to help you invest your bright new treasure." With total insouciance, he sprawled into a chair at their table.

"This man is mad!" Mordermi shook his head. "I think I've seen you before—skulking about the Pit near the waterfront, reeling from the fumes of the yellow lotus. I don't know how you made your way in here, but whether you're Rimanendo's spy or playing your own mad game, you won't find leaving here with our secret as easy a task."

"Secret? Surely you didn't think a theft of this magnitude could be kept secret? Every tongue in the Pit speaks of Mordermi's daring raid of last night. Even the dull wits of Rimanendo's court must know by now whose hand stripped them of their baubles—and their pride. A pity you could not have stolen the one without the other, Mordermi. In the past, Rimanendo has done nothing about you simply because you were never worth his attention. You may be prince of thieves here in the Pit, but His Majesty and his lords steal more from the people in a week's taxes than you and your band could steal from Rimanendo in a year's looting.

"But now you've stolen their pride. Rimanendo can only save face when you and your men are feeding ravens on the Dancing Floor. And worse, you have made an alliance with the White Rose—goading it from sedition to insurrection. Korst will move against the Pit, and Rimanendo will give him authority to use whatever force he requires to destroy Mordermi and the White Rose.

"And so," Callidios concluded. "You'll want to invest

your newfound fortune with extreme care, or you'll soon be boasting of your wealth to the ravens."

"This man is a genius," Mordermi laughed sourly. "Until this moment, we'd thought Rimanendo had *wanted* us to share his wealth. And in the few breaths that you have left, pray tell us how to spend our treasure."

"Use it to destroy Rimanendo—before he destroys you!"

Callidios lurched out of his chair, began to pace the room in his maddeningly disjointed posturing.

"You've stolen a fortune, but you don't know its worth. You talk of food for the starving, fine clothes for yourselves, leaflets to disseminate your political theories, weapons for your followers. You remind me of the theives who stole an ancient amulet from a temple of Set in my homeland. When they were captured, it was found that they had broken loose the gems, melted down the gold—thinking themselves wealthy men, when the amulet they had thus destroyed had the power to make its holder invulnerable.

"Do you know what you have here? You have the price of a kingdom! If you use this wealth intelligently, you can bring about the downfall of Rimanendo. Instead of hunted fugitives hiding in the Pit, you can be the new rulers of all Zingara and live at ease in the palaces of your former masters."

"As you observed," Santiddio nodded to Mordermi, "the man is mad."

"Perhaps he only shares his lotus dreams with us," Mordermi said, "But such dreams are a splendid vision."

"I'll cure his madness," rumbled Conan.

"No, wait!" Mordermi halted him. "Let's hear Callidios out."

"Consider the balance of power that holds Rimanendo's reign together," Callidios went on, as confidently as if they were seated in his chambers. "At the top of the pyramid is King Rimanendo, corrupt and incompetent, his only concern as ruler being that the taxes that fill the royal coffers are sufficient to support his excesses. Below the king are his lords, left to tyrannize the people of Zingara as they will, so long as nothing disturbs Rimanendo's pleasures. Any one of the strongest houses might depose Rimanendo, but for the jealousy of their rivals—who would surely interfere with any change in the balance of power. Supporting the king and his court is the army—both the Royal Zingaran Army and the private armies of the powerful lords. They enforce the will of their masters upon those who make up the base of the pyramid—the people of Zingara.''

"This man," said Santiddio, "has a wonderous obsession to tell us things we already know well.''

"And yet you tolerate this situation," Callidios gibed.

"Not for very much longer!" Carico burst out, unable to contain himself further. "When the base of the pyramid moves, those at the top must fall. The White Rose shall lead the people of Zingara into a new social order in which there are neither oppressors nor oppressed.''

"I'm sure we're all of us here of a like sentiment," Callidios cut him off. "But rhetoric does not overthrow princes, nor do peasants with clubs face down disciplined troops.''

"The soldiers will not fight their brothers, once the White Rose convinces them that our cause is the cause of all the people of Zingara.''

"Wrong, Carico! The soldiers will fight whomever they are paid to fight. That's why they're soldiers.''

Callidios jerked about and pointed to the treasure-laden table.

"They will fight for that.''

Despite themselves, they found that they were listening to the Stygian's words.

"You see in that treasure only material wealth," Callidios continued. "You are like the unfortunate thieves with the amulet. For I tell you that the true value of this treasure is *power!* And more than that, the means to far greater power. Absolute power in Zingara—if you dare.''

"Why don't I test this sorcerer's illusions with honest steel?'' Conan suggested. "His tongue weaves as twisted a course as his pacing.''

"Let him continue,'' Avvinti interceded. "The man may be mad, but he's not a fool.''

"Zingara is ripe for the taking,'' Callidios went on unperturbedly. "But not by oratory and petty theft. Any of the powerful lords could take the throne from Rimanendo—if their rivals would permit it. But usurpation would upset the balance of power and bring about civil war—and civil wars have a way of leaving both factions devastated. So Rimanendo continues to rule.

"But with the power that is now yours—if you choose to wield it—you can upset this balance. Mordermi is a hero to the downtrodden people of Zingara, and the White Rose has the ear of the masses. With this wealth you can buy powerful friends, win the attention of those in high places. You can bribe the king's judges, buy favors from court officials. You can buy weapons and mail for your people's army, or better by far, hire companies of veteran mercenaries to fight for you. Once your power is recognized, you can form secret alliances with the great lords. Then you will be strong enough to strike at Rimanendo and his followers—and from the flames of civil war, a new order and a new ruler can be forged by your will.

"The moment for greatness is yours to seize. Hesitate, and that moment will be lost forever, and you will be destroyed by the powers you have already called forth.''

"And exactly where do you fit into this glorious dream?'' Santiddio wanted to know.

"I expect to share in your power, obviously,'' Callidios told him suavely. "As Mordermi has observed, I am a man of subtle talents. After all, I strolled into your hidden fortress without hindrance from your formidable crew of cutthroats. I can stroll out again—taking your treasure with me, if I needed such trifles. But my design is to seize a kingdom, not to snarl amidst the other dogs for the bones that are tossed from the king's table.''

"All very bold, this design of yours," Mordermi said. "But I fail to see why we need a renegade Stygian sorcerer to help us carry it out. One wonders that a man of your self-proclaimed abilities should spend his days here in the Pit.''

Callidios made a lopsided shrug. "As you have guessed, it would not be good for me to return to Stygia. Nor am I any lord of the Black Ring, or you'd not see me in this low state. But I have my reasons for biding my days prowling about the Pit.''

He poured himself a chalice of wine as he talked, fell back into his chair, somehow without spilling a drop of wine.

"My father was a priest of Set; my mother was an Æsir slave who was purchased to perform some central functions in a certain sacrificial rite. She was beautiful, my father lusted for her, and in a short time she was no longer acceptable for any ritual of virgin sacrifice. My father was powerful enough to escape discipline for his actions, but not disgrace. When I was born not long afterward, his enemies considered me beneath their attentions, while my father saw me as a reminder of his fall from grace.

"My mother died. I was allowed to wander about the temples like a wild thing—tolerated much the way a stray dog is given run of a kitchen, so long as he remains unobtrusive. I learned many things in the temples of Set—absorbing secrets and forbidden knowledge just as a stray seeks out crumbs and scraps unnoticed by its indifferent keepers. In time it became essential for me to depart from Stygia, but not before I had mastered sufficient powers to make good my escape. That I sit here before you now is proof that I do not make idle boast.

"From Luxur I fled to Khemi, and there took ship to Kordava. For some weeks now I have lived here in the Pit, but not because I sought to hide—this buried city would be no refuge against those who would seek me out if they could. Rather, I came to the Pit seeking to find certain things of which I had knowledge. I found that which I sought, but was uncertain what use to make of my knowledge. Of course, every citizen of the Pit knows of the daring exploits of Mordermi. Once I learned of last night's little coup, I saw how we two might serve one another to considerable mutual advantage."

"Callidios, I'll say this," Mordermi laughed. "For a self-taught sorcerer, you have as much effrontery as any rogue I've known. If your spells were half as alluring as your words, you'd rule Stygia today. Still, there's some sense in what you've said, and I can always use another clever rogue in my band. Can you really use that sword, or do you first ensorcell your opponents to sleep before running them through?"

"As to that, I really can't judge," Callidios said quietly. "But I can raise an army of swordsmen no human opponent would care to face."

"An army?" Mordermi wondered if he should laugh. There was an icy confidence to Callidios' tone that no longer struck him as amusing.

"An army that I can summon forth by my secret knowledge," Callidios told him. "Just as you can summon an army by means of the wealth you have stolen. Shall we be allies, Mordermi, you and I?"

Mordant laughter flickered in those gray-green eyes, so that Mordermi wondered suddenly which of them played the fool.

VIII.   A Morning Swim

The sea washed sluggishly against the snarl of rotted piers.
At a distance, Conan could hear the roll of bells. He watched
Sandokazi as she thrust her bare legs into the leaden waters,
and wondered whether this could be heaven or might be hell.

"We'll need a boat," Callidios had said. "And someone
to row it. And someone who's a strong swimmer."

Conan drew back on the oars with a sour grunt that sent
the boat sliding through the low swells. In the stern, Sandokazi hitched her skirts over her thighs and kicked at their
wake. In the bow, Callidios struck contorted attitudes and
shouted fitful instructions. Conan had agreed to go on this
excursion with the half-formed notion of tying the anchor
to the Stygian's neck and throwing him overboard in the
deepest part of the bay.

Mordermi and Santiddio were deep in schemes with the
outlaw's chief henchmen and the inner circle of the White
Rose; had been throughout the night. To Conan's uncon-
cealed disgust, they had accepted the Stygian's ideas
wholeheartedly—so much so that Mordermi already declared (and perhaps believed) that Callidios had but seconded
his own private thoughts.

Moreover, Callidios had spoken of certain potent sorceries
that were his to command—wondrous powers that he might

summon to aid the cause of his newfound comrades. Lotus dreams, perhaps. But it is never prudent to ignore the claims of one who has been privy to the abhorrent secrets of the priests of Set. Callidios professed to be able to demonstrate proof of his bold assertion; Conan was detailed to examine such proofs, and Sandokazi joined their party to forstall Conan's hostile designs upon a potentially useful ally.

The morning was yet cool beneath the diminishing sea mists, although the speed with which the climbing sun melted the gray veil betokened the clear, hot day that awaited them. Conan, remembering that Korst would be watching the harbor, again cursed Callidios for this madman's excursion onto the bay of Kordava. The tide was at ebb, and a motley confusion of merchant vessels and fishing boats put out to sea this morning, so that Conan felt some confidence that their skiff would draw no notice.

"Conan, look!" Sandokazi called out. "You can see people down there on the bottom!"

Callidios all but went over the side in his haste to see where she pointed. "Statues!" he snapped querulously. "Nothing but garden statuary. I'll show you better than that."

Conan rested his oars and looked over the side. As the morning sunlight penetrated the blue depths, the sunken ruins of old Kordava could be discerned some fathoms below them. Half-buried beneath a forest of seaweed, a cluster of broken statuary stood watch amidst the toppled columns and broken walls of a drowned villa. Schools of small fish shimmered like flights of silver birds about the encrusted stones and jumbles of corroded brick. Dimly, other reefs of ruined structures merged into the inverted horizon, where long streamers of seaweed waved in the current as if stirred by a morning breeze.

"I hadn't realized so much of the old city had dropped beneath the sea during the earthquake," Conan mused. "I thought only a section along the waterfront slid into the sea, but we must be close to a mile offshore here.''

"We're beyond the walls of the old city here," Callidios told him. "This was once a long peninsula that enclosed part of what was then Kordava's harbor. The entire peninsula sank beneath the sea when the earthquake struck this coast. The wealthy had their villas here; we're passing over the remains of one now."

He squinted toward the open sea, where the running tide fretted across the submerged bar of land. "Good, we're on course. Keep rowing along the shoal here. The tomb lies farther to sea, but we'll have no trouble finding it at low tide."

"Is it a tomb you're leading us to, then?" Conan asked sarcastically. "I thought you were going to show us your army."

"I'll show you as much as you'll care to see, Cimmerian."

Conan spat into the sea and took up the oars. The Cimmerian had given little thought and less credence to Callidios' boasts. He entertained a vague notion that the Stygian renegade might have some sort of cutthroat band under his command—possibly waiting offshore aboard ship, or lurking upon one of the small islands at the delta of the Black River where it emptied into the sea at Kordava.

"Whose tomb do we seek?" Sandokazi asked, to break the silence.

"That of King Kalenius."

Sandokazi pursed her lips in thought. "King of lotus dreams, perhaps. I don't recall the name 'Kalenius' amongst the kings of Zingara."

Conan snorted, thinking that the water would be very deep once they were beyond this shoal.

"Kalenius was one of the greatest of the Thurian kings," Callidios informed them loftily. "His was an age when Atlantis and Lemuria yet rose above the waves, and the kingdoms of this land were Verulia and Farsun and Valusia, and Zingara was a realm whose birth awaited another millennium.''

"Well, I've never heard of this Kalenius," Sandokazi said petulantly. "Nor his kingdom, nor his tomb."

"The kings and kingdoms of ancient Thuria are ghosts and dust, forgotten by the proud Hyborian civilization that has arisen above the bones of their greatness," Callidios sneered. "I think there will come a day when our age, too, shall pass into dust, and the children who dance upon our bones shall remember our lands and our races only in their dreams."

"What rot!" Sandokazi laughed. "Kings may die, but how can this land and its peoples pass away?"

"Look beneath our wake for your answer," Callidios returned.

Conan forbore comment. If Sandokazi chose to bandy words with a madman, it was her amusement. A few lengths of anchor rope and a hundred fathoms would soon still Callidios' tongue.

"In the centuries after Kull the Atlantean seized the throne of Valusia and plunged the Thurian kingdoms into an age of internecine warfare, it was Kalenius who finally brought the peace of conquest to the lands north and west of Grondar and the Lost Lands. Kalenius' was an empire beyond the dreams of even the ambitious Prince Yezdigerd of Turan. The rulers and peoples of a continent bowed their necks to his will and his whim. Kalenius declared that his empire should last a thousand years and his fame throughout eternity.

"But Kalenius grew old and died; his empire shattered into civil wars even as the king was laid within his tomb. Finally the Cataclysm drew a veil of darkness over the kingdoms of Thuria, and the fame of Kalenius is remembered only by those few who seek out the lost knowledge of a lost age.''

Callidios broke off his monologue with an abrupt shift of stance, and shouted wildly: "Hold your oars, Conan! We are here!"

In another instant, the Stygian had thrown over the anchor. His crooked grin met Conan's eyes, and Conan cursed silently.

They rode at anchor perhaps a league from shore. At low tide, the shoal here lay but a fathom beneath their skiff. Choppy waves foamed the surface above the sunken peninsula, and Conan guessed the currents would be treacherous with the turning of the tide. No other vessels were within hailing distance—their masters keeping to the deeper waters.

"Below us," gestured Callidios, "the tomb of King Kalenius."

Conan and Sandokazi peered dutifully. The sea was clear, but the wave-flecked shallows made it difficult to see below the surface. Gulls wheeled and cried overhead; the wind and sea grated together. Conan sensed that the bottom had risen here at the terminus of the shoal, indicating a sunken knoll of considerable expanse.

"What tomb?" Conan asked, glancing significantly at Sandokazi.

"Beneath the sea and beneath the sand," Callidios replied. "A thousand years ago, and you might have discerned the ruins of some of the larger funereal monuments of the mausoleum upon which Kalenius lavished thirty years' construction. What the Cataclysm spared, the founding fathers of Kordava hauled away for building stone. Only the barrow yet stood, and at last the sea swallowed up even that. We're anchored atop all that remains of that barrow."

"Fascinating," lied Sandokazi.

"Thirty years Kalenius devoted to the building of his

87

tomb. A hundred thousand skilled laborers, ten thousand master artisans, the riches of an empire—directed by the will of the absolute ruler of the Thurian continent to build for him a tomb that would be the wonder of the world, a tomb that would outlast the ages.''

"I'm sure there's a lesson here for us all,'' Sandokazi yawned. The sun was growing hot, and the morning's adventure had worn thin.

"There's *nothing* here,'' Conan corrected her, feeling cheated after the Stygian's grandiose speech.

Callidios was tugging off his boots. "There is, if you know where to look. Marble temples and golden fountains may have outlasted the ages no more than a wreath of flowers tossed upon a grave, but the paramount wonders of King Kalenius' tomb were hidden beneath the earth.''

Callidios laid his boots beside his rapier, spread his doublet atop the pile, and began to wriggle out of trunk hose. "Of course,'' he looked up at the Cimmerian, "you'll have to swim a bit, if you want to see for yourself.''

Conan shrugged, and kicked off his boots. He was already stripped to the waist, and in a moment he had dragged his legs free of trousers. About his naked waist he belted his dagger, taking care that it was snug in its sheath.

Sandokazi smiled at him boldly, then began to unlace her bodice. Stepping out of her skirts, she drew her blouse over her head and faced him wearing only her thin cotton shift.

"You're coming along?'' Conan half objected.

"Why not? It's a fine morning for a swim, and Callidios has promised to show us 'paramount wonders.' ''

"We won't be long at this,'' Callidios said, adjusting the anchor rope so that they floated across the edge of the submerged knoll. Stripped, the Stygian seemed a mismatched assortment of knobby joints and angular limbs. Beside Conan's sun-bronzed, broadly muscled frame, Callidios resembled an undernourished alley cat that had just crawled out of a puddle.

"What are we supposed to see?" Conan demanded.

"Just follow me," Callidios evaded, and tumbled into the sea.

Laughing gaily, Sandokazi dived into the sea after him. Frowning, Conan followed.

Three heads bobbed above the open sea. Behind them, the empty skiff rode its anchor in the morning breeze. Callidios, his tow-colored locks plastered muddily against his domelike skull, dog-paddled out to where the bottom fell suddenly away. Treading water, he awaited the other two swimmers.

"The thousand-columned mausoleum with its ceiling panes of lapis lazuli across which a golden sun traversed by day and a platina moon by night, and its paving tiles of serpentine through which rivers of quicksilver coursed, was meant to be no more than a gaudy display for generations of mourning subjects. The flesh of King Kalemius, preserved through the arcana of his sorcerers, was laid to rest beneath the earth, in a secret tomb whose marvels surpassed those of his mausoleum even as the edifice overawed a pauper's grave. From the level plain, Kalenius commanded his subjects to bring forth a mountain. Two hundred thousand slaves toiled for three decades, carrying earth to raise for Kalenius a mountain where no mountain had stood before.

"It was a barrow worthy to enshrine a dead god. Two hundred feet above the plain it rose, a circular tumulus a thousand feet in breadth. Upon its height were raised the temples and funerary monuments to daze the imagination of his subjects. But within its depths was buried a palace more lavish than that from which King Kalenius ruled a continent, wherein the king's mortal remains were placed upon a golden throne to rule in the afterworld for eternity."

Callidios paused for breath. Conan cast a wary glance toward the skiff, saw that its anchor held, and thought that the Stygian might have offered this grandiloquent speech before jumping overboard.

"At the time when the earth shook and destroyed old Kordava," Callidios continued, "Kalenius was a name forgotten, and his barrow was no more than an inconsequential knoll. Then the sea swallowed up all that remained of one of the greatest works of the Pre-Cataclysmic Age, and the mountain that a king had raised was reduced to a nameless shoal. Riven by Cataclysm and earthquake, the hidden tomb of Kalenius sank beneath the sea, where now the tides and storms of more than a century have relentlessly stripped away the final barrier to his subterranean palace. If you'll see proof of my words, then follow me."

Conan grew suddenly interested in spite of his skepticism. The prospect of a royal tomb for the looting made his thoughts race with the possibilities. King Kalenius' gold, if not his fame, would have outlasted the ages.

"This tomb . . ." Conan began.

But Callidios had already doubled over and vanished beneath the waves.

Conan sucked in his breath with a curse and twisted in a surface dive to follow the Stygian into the depths.

The salt water stung his eyes at first, but once the blur left his vision, he could see quite well. Close beside him, Conan caught sight of Sandokazi—her white shift translucent as it pressed and swirled about her lithe figure. Ahead of them, Callidios was swimming out past the edge of the sunken knoll, diving deeper still. The pressure began to lancinate his skull, but Conan set his teeth and swam after the sorcerer.

The bottom fell away quickly, once they were past the shoal. Writhing tangles of seaweed shrouded the submarine slope, making its exact contours impossible to define. Conan caught vague outlines of huge slabs of stone, skewed out from the sea bottom in irregular order. Looking closer, he thought he could make out the cylindrical outcroppings of broken columns.

Conan's chest was tight, his skull compressed with pain, when Callidios hovered above a sudden patch of blackness against the sunken slope. The Stygian gestured frenziedly downward, then shot toward the surface. Using the last of his breath, Conan swam closer to where Callidios had pointed.

Festooned by waving strands of weed, a fissure gaped darkly from the face of the sunken knoll. A talus of stone slabs and truncated columns spilled away from the fissure and downward along the slope into the murky depths of the former shoreline. As he swam past the opening, Conan saw that it penetrated the tumulus beyond the limits of his vision. Half-blocked with muck and debris, the mouth of the tunnel was flanked by a row of stone figures, vaguely glimpsed against the blackness within.

His lungs thirsting for air, Conan turned quickly for the surface. Protruding from the wall of sunlight above, he could see Callidios' bony legs treading the water, and next to him Sandokazi's shapely limbs—temptingly displayed as her shift floated upward. Conan surfaced beside them, sucking in a huge breath of air.

"Well?" Callidios demanded. "Did you see?"

"I saw stone ruins and a cave in the side of the bar," Conan rumbled, wiping at his eyes. The skiff bobbed in the waves not far from where they now swam.

"Just as I told you," the Stygian exulted. "Sea and earthquake have at last broken open the barrow, and the passage into King Kalenius' tomb is laid bare. I spent long days out here in search of this passage, seeking proof that it was indeed his tomb—and have I not found it? Did you not see? Was I not right?"

"You claimed to know of some mysterious army that you could summon to help us overthrow Rimanendo," Conan reminded him. "We came out here to see proof of that boast, and instead you show us drowned ruins and a sunken barrow. It comes to me that your promise to aid us is an empty boast, and what you really want is our help in seeking questionable loot in an underwater tomb."

"Did you think I would have shared this knowledge with you and your cutthroat friends if I didn't need your help?" Callidios chided. "The tomb holds riches beyond your dreams, Cimmerian—or I'd never have fled Stygia to seek it out. But I said I'd show you proof of the powers I can command for you. Think again. What else did you see down below?"

"Nothing but a hole in the mud and broken columns," Conan repeated. "And some statues, like those we passed earlier."

"Statues?" Callidios laughed. "You saw them then? Examine them more closely this time, Cimmerian."

Without wait for argument, Callidios again made a surface dive and plunged into the depths. Wondering what mad jest the Stygian played, Conan followed suit.

Again the lancing agony within his skull as the pressure of the depths closed upon him. Conan judged that only a skilled diver would be capable of reaching this fissure except at low tide. That the Stygian had been able to locate the submerged cave was an achievement that earned Conan's grudging respect—albeit, what game the sorcerer played remained an enigma to him.

Callidios swam slowly above the dark opening in the side of the underwater ridge. Although the forest of seaweed obscured the bottom, from the position of the stone ruins Conan decided that the Stygian had spoken the truth: that the earthquake coupled with the action of the sea had broken open a barrow whose hidden tomb must have been of royal magnitude.

Swimming closer to the mouth of the passage, Conan glanced at the statues that stood within, half-buried in debris and seaweed. They were life-size figures of warriors, bearing weapons and armor of archaic and unfamiliar pattern, cunningly sculpted with careful attention to detail from some glossy black stone that had resisted the cerements of barnacles and seagrowths that encrusted the stone ruins. There were half a dozen or more of them arrayed near the tunnel mouth, and others dimly visible farther within. The craftsmanship was exquisite, and assuming they could be raised, they would doubtless fetch a good price in Kordava. This then: the army of Callidios' jest. Fantastic riches might indeed lie within the drowned barrow, but these were safe from any thief who lacked gills. No wonder Callidios had sought help in despoiling this tomb he had discovered.

Sandokazi swam past him for a better look at the Stygian's discovery. Her tanned legs thrust powerfully as she reached the mouth of the passage and hovered close to the foremost of the stone warriors.

The statue's arm shot out. An onyx fist closed upon her shift.

Sandokazi had started for the surface. She glanced down to see what her shift had caught upon. A scream stole a torrent of bubbles from her mouth.

Holding Sandokazi fast, the statue lifted a stone mace in its other hand, dragged the struggling girl toward itself. Scarcely slowed by the enveloping sea, the mace swept down for her head in a killing blow.

Not losing time to seek to comprehend, Conan drew his knife and lunged downward for the writhing figure of the girl. Catching her by the shoulder, he jerked her body aside just as the mace slashed past them.

From the corner of his eye, Conan saw that another of the black stone figures was turning toward them. Seamuck churned from half-buried legs as it shuddered forth from the passage—onyx sword raised to strike.

The trail of bubbles from Sandokazi's mouth ceased, as her limbs thrashed in helpless frenzy. Conan's knife stabbed against the black arm that pinioned her—its steel blade skidded harmlessly against adamantine stone. The mace smashed toward him. Conan doubled up, evaded the blow—kicking savagely against the stone shoulder in an effort to drag free.

The girl's cotton shift tore apart in the struggle, freeing her abruptly. Under the impetus of his thrust, Conan flung away from the stone warrior—clutching Sandokazi's naked form.

Holding the half-drowned girl in his arms, Conan kicked frantically toward the surface. He risked one quick glance downward. The stone warrior glared upward at them from the tunnel mouth, mace upraised and a rag of Sandokazi's shift in the other black fist—proof that his had not been some nightmarish delusion of the depths.

Conan broke water. Sandokazi retched and fought for breath, still struggling in mindless panic.

"Callidios, you treacherous bastard!" Conan snarled. "You knew those things were alive! Why didn't you warn us!"

"I knew they'd start to move when you approached them," the Stygian defended himself. "But they're far too heavy to swim up to us, after all, and I never thought you'd be careless enough to swim within their reach."

Callidios smiled maliciously. "Where's that sneering condescension now, my friends? So! Am I a mad lotus-dreamer? You thought me nothing more than that a moment ago. Why waste my wisdom on a doubting barbarian lout and a supercilious trull? I told you I could summon an army through my secret knowledge; you doubted and demanded proof of my claim. I have shown you proof as required, and if the demonstration was not without certain dangers, I shared them with you."

"Oh, leave him alone, Conan," Sandokazi urged between coughs. "He's right. We wouldn't have believed him, if we hadn't seen for ourselves. I wanted to see what stone they were carved from, or I wouldn't have blundered into the thing's reach."

Conan cursed him fervently, but the sorcerer kept his distance, and Sandokazi was still too shaken to swim without Conan's help. Vowing to settle the account at another time, the Cimmerian made for the skiff.

As quickly as they could, the three swimmers reached the rowboat and clambered on board.

"You still could have warned us," Conan repeated angrily. His blue eyes smouldered dangerously as he hauled in the anchor.

Sandokazi, still coughing up sea water, cast an uneasy glance over the side. Maybe the stone warriors couldn't swim, but she wished Conan would forget Callidios and start rowing. She was shivering, although the sun was hot.

"What are those things?" she wondered.

"They were called the Final Guard," Callidios answered. "One thousand of the finest warriors in all Kalenius' empire—fanatics who swore loyalty to their king through oaths that not even death might cancel."

"Those were no human warriors!" Conan protested. "The arm I struck turned my dagger blade as if its flesh were stone."

"Once it was living flesh," Callidios told him. "But Kalenius knew that no mortal flesh could guard his tomb throughout the ages. Hidden chambers must ultimately yield their secrets to the patient; subtle pitfalls betray themselves even as they strike; deadly spells may be countered by more potent sorceries: these Kalenius knew would be insufficient to defend his eternal palace from thieves and interlopers.

"His archimages created the Final Guard. In order that Kalenius' tomb should remain guarded throughout the ages, one thousand of his elite warriors were transformed into deathless creatures of living stone. For millennia have they kept their watch beneath the earth, while continents reeled and sank, and Kalenius and his empire passed into legend and faded from memory. As you have seen, they are still at their post."

"How could any man have chosen such a fate!" Sandokazi shuddered, struggling into her clothes as the sun dried her skin.

"History doesn't record whether they were given their choice in the matter," Callidios shrugged. "It is not uncommon that a great monarch should ordain that his household be entombed with him—either living or slain. The Final Guard was an elite regiment comprised of fanatics who considered it an honor to be chosen. And, after all, while other rulers allow their soldiers to die for them, Kalenius bestowed instead a certain immortality upon the warriors of the Final Guard."

"You call living death an honor?" Conan snorted, pulling vigorously at the oars.

"But you'll have to agree they've performed their duty without fail," Callidios said. "The hand of time may have reduced Kalenius' eternal palace to a drowned ruin, but his tomb has never been despoiled by any human thieves. How can any man prevail against guardians such as these? Steel cannot slay them; gold cannot corrupt them. Only Kalenius can command them, and Kalenius is dead. Kalenius commanded them to defend his eternal palace, and the Final Guard will obey that command until time itself comes to an end."

Conan stopped rowing. "So you have brought us out here to show us an army of devils that no man can control, and a royal tomb that no man can plunder. Mordermi will not thank you for this.''

''Mordermi will indeed thank me when I accomplish both of these things,'' Callidios said confidently.

''Conan!'' Sandokazi broke in. ''There's a fire on the waterfront!''

Conan turned to see where she pointed. A plume of dark smoke had begun to climb into the cloudless sky. Then, elsewhere along the waterfront, other tendrils of gray suddenly crawled up from squalid buildings there. Conan shaded his eyes with his hand and peered intently. The sun and rising flames glinted from the tiny figures that milled about the distant streets.

''It's Korst!'' Conan said grimly. ''He's attacking the Pit!''

IX. No Road Back

Korst's attack was a move born of desperation.

Following Mordermi's raid, King Rimanendo had summoned his general to his presence. Rimanendo had expressed his royal will with unwonted terseness: "If, in three days, these thieves are not hanged, you will be."

That Mordermi was the mastermind behind the outrage was a discovery that would have yielded to a spy network far less capable than that which General Korst employed. Heretofore the daring outlaw had been little more than an annoyance to Korst—Mordermi's depredations were a matter for the city guard, and not the army's concern. The raid on the king's pavilion changed all that. Rimanendo's honor had been insulted, and the participation of the White Rose betokened open insurrection. Recovery of the loot was secondary; Mordermi and his band must be annihilated at any cost.

And Korst knew full well that that cost would be high. The Pit was a city within Kordava—a realm where Zingara's laws were of no more consequence than those of Khitai or Vendhya. To move against the Pit was to invade a foreign land, and the citizens of the Pit were certain to make a bloody resistance to Rimanendo's authority.

Korst did not intend to stand in Mordermi's stead upon the Dancing Floor.

By the time Conan reached the waterfront, Korst's attack was well underway. The burgundy and gold of the Royal Zingaran Army seemed to flow through the streets. Buildings above the area of the Pit leaked smoke and flame, while tight knots of men bottlenecked at the chief entrances to the sunken city.

"You're not going into that?" Callidios asked.

"Mordermi is my friend," Conan stated simply. To the Cimmerian his course of action was unalterable.

"Mordermi is caught in a trap," Callidios said. "You'll have to battle through Korst's lines for the dubious privilege of joining your friends in a last stand."

"I'd be with them now, if you hadn't led us on a pointless chase," Conan growled. "If Mordermi can hold out long enough to stall Korst's attack, there's a chance for us. Korst won't dare lay waste to half of Kordava just to smoke us out."

He added: "Sandokazi, you'd be better off clear of this. You and Callidios take the skiff once I've reached shore, and try to . . ."

"If you think I'm going to run out, you're as mad as Callidios," Sandokazi broke in. "This is my fight more than it is yours, Conan."

"As you wish," Conan shrugged. Cimmerian women were never ones to shy from bloodshed, although he had observed that the civilized races demanded a certain timidity of their women.

"Callidios," he went on, "as soon as we touch shore, you can row back to Stygia for all I care."

The sorcerer had pulled on his garments and was buckling on his rapier. "I told Mordermi I'd make him a king," he grinned. "It's unfortunate that General Korst has stolen a march on us, but there's no question of turning back now—

for any of us, it seems. You and your friends have talked about a revolution. Well, you've started one now, and for rebels there is no quarter. If we're to be hailed as liberators and not hanged as traitors, we must trust to our swords now—and to our wits.''

Which made Callidios' chances just about nil, Conan judged. The Stygian renegade was a puzzle to him. Was there truly courage behind those sardonic eyes, or had the fumes of the yellow lotus made him oblivious to physical danger? Conan gave the matter up, and looked to his broadsword.

Sandokazi had a thought. ''Callidios, you were able to spirit yourself into our headquarters last night. Can you work your magic now to get us through Korst's cordon?''

''Get the three of us through this melee in broad daylight?'' the Stygian protested. ''The situation is entirely different. Would you also expect a master of thimbelrig to be able to turn base metals into gold? If I had such powers, I wouldn't be here now.''

''I think we at last hear a true confession of this sorcerer's boasted powers,'' Conan sneered.

''What do you know of sorcery, Cimmerian?'' Callidios bristled. ''If a warrior is a master archer, does it follow that he is equally skilled with the sword? I have followed certain paths, and others I have not followed—yet there is no lord of the Black Ring who has delved farther along the paths I have chosen.''

''Tell that to the first of Korst's Strikers who asks your business here,'' Conan suggested. ''We'll try to reach Mordermi through the tunnel we used after the raid. Korst can't have men watching every rathole.''

In this much Conan was right. It was a dilemma that General Korst fully appreciated. Instead, Korst had thrown a street-level cordon about the approximate boundaries of the Pit, then had dispatched three companies of the Royal

Zingaran Army into the subterranean city. With King Rimanendo giving him a free hand to deal with Mordermi's band, Korst intended to treat the Pit as an enemy stronghold. Those who made no resistance would be taken prisoner—to be released or arrested pending subsequent investigation. Those who resisted were in open defiance of martial law and of the king's will; they were to be crushed without mercy.

If all went well, Korst would have Mordermi bottled up in his lair, would overpower his men almost before the outlaws realized they were under attack. Korst was realist enough to know that the odds were against so easy a victory; that more likely he would have all the citizens of the Pit in arms against the king's soldiers. No matter. Korst was prepared to use any amount of force necessary to capture Mordermi, and the lives of the rabble meant no more to Korst than to his royal master.

The tunnel from the waterfront had escaped Korst's attention and passed them beneath his cordon. How long it might remain undiscovered, Conan couldn't guess—but he knew better than to count on it as an avenue to escape. With Sandokazi and Callidios in tow, the Cimmerian forced his way through the press, hoping to reach Mordermi's stronghold before Korst's soldiers overran the Pit.

Conan surged across a battlefield alien to any of his experience. Beneath the streets of Kordava, the Pit was a claustrophobic maze of carnage and mayhem, more resembling a sprawling tavern brawl than a pitched battle. There was no open space—only streets and buildings crushed with struggling and frenzied humanity, while overhead a pall of smoke lowered the vaulted ceiling of the Pit. The air choked his lungs; the tumult deafened his ears. Conan had once seen two armies of ants locked in battle upon an anthill, had broken open the mound to marvel at the ferocious combat that attacker and defender waged within its tunnels. That memory came to him now, as he shouldered through the congested alleys of the buried city.

It was chaos more than any armed resistance that impeded their progress. Having surrounded the Pit, Korst had invaded the underground city from three points, intending to secure the area before its inhabitants had time to react. But the Pit took warning with the first appearance of the cordon, and the presence of the Royal Zingaran Army convinced all within that Rimanendo intended to cleanse Kordava of its infamous sink of vice and crime, as had long been threatened. Desperate, unable to flee, the denizens of the Pit fought back like cornered rats.

Expecting no more resistance from the populace than from a mass of frightened sheep, Korst's vanguard instead encountered savage beasts. These were no helpless law-abiding citizens, accustomed to respond blindly to the commands of authority. The people of the Pit were rogues and hardened criminals, heavily armed men to whom violence was a fact of life—who hated the king's laws only less than they hated those who enforced them. Korst's men had not penetrated very far into the narrow streets, before they found their way blocked by barricades and mobs of desperate men and women. Arrows and stones struck invisibly into their ordered ranks, as the walls of the overhanging buildings gave protection to snipers within. The soldiers bogged down upon their own dead and wounded, unable to progress along the close confines of the tunnel-like streets. Retreating as best they could, they sent word to Korst that any ordered advance was impossible. Korst, unimpressed, attacked with fresh troops.

Into this impasse, Conan and his companions fought their way. The perimeter secured, Korst's soldiers battled without success to force an entrance into the Pit. Within, a state of siege existed—as the denizens of the Pit united to defend their city from an invader whose triumph would surely mean their extinction. Fires raged out of control along the periphery—threatening to spread conflagration throughout Kordava. Men and women raced through the streets, carrying weapons and material to barricade all passages that gave entrance into the Pit. Behind the barricades and in the cramped alleyways, a grim and ugly struggle to the death flung up new barriers of butchered flesh.

They had almost reached Mordermi's stronghold, when Conan caught sight of the outlaw leader mounted amidst a circle of his men. Mordermi's face was flushed with excitement, but he gave no evidence of panic as he deliberately gave orders for the defense of his realm. His lips made a quick smile, as he answered Conan's hail.

"There's a Cimmerian for you!" Mordermi laughed. "While some of my bold rogues talk of fleeing, Conan comes rushing back looking for a fight. What did you find out?"

"Korst has the Pit surrounded . . ." Conan began.

"Tell me something I don't know. We'll give Korst a belly full! We're holding our own against his assault, and Santiddio has the White Rose up in arms to man the barricades. Korst's attack won far more recruits for their people's army than ever did their long-winded speeches. If we hold the barricades, Korst can't dig us out without tearing down most of Kordava, and not even Rimanendo will give him leave to go that far."

Mordermi nodded toward Callidios. "I meant, what did you find out about our self-announced kingmaker? Did he show you anything worth mentioning, or did you just go chasing after yellow lotus?"

"Ask Sandokazi," Conan snorted, in no mood to talk of sorcery when the smell of battle was in his nostrils. "Where do you want me?"

"Take command of the barricades at Eel Street, and send Sifino to report back to me," Mordermi told him, touching

104

his bandaged left shoulder with a scowl. "Korst is concentrating his forces there, and if he makes a breakthrough he can penetrate the Pit in strength. I'll coordinate the defense from here—with this shoulder I'm not worth a damn in close fighting—and we'll fall back to my stronghold if we have to. It will be better for us if we can keep Korst out of the Pit."

"Now tell me something I don't know," Conan returned. "And give me one of those horses, or I'll miss the fight before I can push through the mob."

One of Mordermi's men dismounted and tossed his reins to Conan. The Cimmerian swung into the saddle and wheeled the horse toward Eel Street—anxious to clear his brain of Callidios' scheme and sorceries by plunging headlong into red battle. Man against man, steel against steel—Conan asked for no more subtle game than this.

Mordermi grinned as he watched the Cimmerian ride through the press. "Mitra! Give me a hundred such men, and Zingara will have a new king!"

He felt Callidios' gaze upon him. "Well, Stygian?" he asked curtly.

"Conan rides to battle, as a good pawn should," Callidios smiled. "Such pawns are useful to win battles, and such battles to win wars—but the man who knows how to make use of his pawns and his victories is the man who follows the road of kings. I think it is time, Mordermi, for the two of us to talk further upon such matters."

X. White Heat

Eel Street—again the pun was typical of Zingaran humor—was as close an approximation to a main thoroughfare as the Pit could boast. In the days of old Kordava, the avenue had borne another name—now forgotten—and had been a wide, straight passage between proud buildings. This day—when most streets within the Pit would scarcely pass two carts abreast—Eel Street offered Korst his best point of assault, and, as his advance faltered elsewhere, the king's general concentrated his attack here.

"Conan!" A familiar voice hailed him from a group of wounded. "You're a welcome sight! Santiddio said you'd gone fishing."

Carico was tying a dirty bandage about one massive thigh. "Bastard just got a nip out of me below my hauberk," he half apologized, as Conan dismounted. "But then, he's not complaining about where I scattered his brains."

"Where is Santiddio?" Conan asked the smith.

"Lit out the back door," Carico said, trying his weight on his wounded leg. "Going to try to rally the new city to our fight. Been better if I'd gone to talk to them, but this sort of work here takes more meat than Santiddio has on his bones."

"Mordermi wanted me to take over the defense here,"

Conan told him. "Where's Sifino?" Down the smoke-filled street, the sounds of combat sounded like rolling thunder.

"Dead, most likely," Carico said. "He was at the first barricade, and that's fallen. Korst is throwing all he'd got at us. You'll need some mail. Take mine. My forge is close by, and I'll send a boy for my other coat of mail, while I staunch this damned scratch. Not many men of our build you can pick from." He nodded toward a row of the slain.

Conan muttered a hasty thanks and dragged Carico's padded gambeson and hauberk over his torso. The stocky blacksmith was shorter than Conan, but his shoulders and girth gave away nothing to the hulking Cimmerican. Carico's gift was no casual gesture: without mail no warrior could long survive this close infighting, and Conan would have had little chance of finding mail large enough to fit his huge frame.

Daylight poured through from the mouth of Eel Street, to some extent obscured by a collapsed pile of masonry and smouldering rubble, where one of the topside buildings had crumpled in flame. This afforded the defenders a moment's respite, while Korst's soldiers were driven back by the heat. Close to the burning rubble, men dragged bodies away from a barricade—overrun, to judge from the burgundy and gold clad bodies that lay between it and a second barricade farther within the Pit. Conan paused here briefly, watched the frantic efforts to strengthen the makeshift fortifications: carts, doors, timbers and large pieces of furniture formed a bulwark from wall to wall, pavement to ceiling. Unlike any ordinary barricade, there was no climbing over one such as this; the invaders would have to smash through it. A gap in the second barricade let men pass through to the fallen one.

"Carry some of this forward," Conan ordered. "We can man the first barricade while Korst regroups, then fall back here if we're driven back. No sense in giving up any more ground to the bastards than we have to. And start a third barricade farther back. Archers—take up positions where you can rake their front as they advance, then fall back to the next barricade and be ready to cover our retreat if they break through.''

The defenders here—Conan guessed their number to be several hundreds—were most of them ordinary citizens, with the remainder partly from Mordermi's band and the rest members of the White Rose who had come here with Carico. If any of them wondered at taking orders from the young Cimmerian, none grumbled aloud. Conan was well liked and respected by those who knew him by acquaintance or reputation; to the others, the mailed giant with the broadsword posed too formidable a figure to tempt any to question his leadership.

Conan retrieved a steel burgonet from a heap of the slain, and pulled it down over his head. Casting about, he scavenged a serviceable buckler from the same source. Men hastened to shore up the outermost of the barricades—flinging the dead onto the bulwark. This was like fighting in a cavern, Conan reflected—gloomy and cramped. It would be a brutal, inelegant combat—scarcely the stuff of romantic ballads. Notwithstanding, a certain calmness dominated his thoughts. The mores and motives of his civilized friends might baffle Conan, but when civilization shed its sophistication and sought to settle the issue through force of arms, Conan was in his element.

Beyond the smouldering barrier of the collapsed building, Conan could see Zingaran soldiers working to douse the flames and clear a path through the rubble. Those of their fellows who had been cut off by the cave-in had fallen to the regrouping defenders. Probably Korst's men would otherwise have succeeded in making their breakthrough here.

As figures took shape through the smoke-filled passage, rebel archers loosed their bows. Advancing behind their shields, Korst's men stumbled and wavered beneath the punishing barrage—deadly at pointblank range. But more soldiers forced past the bodies of their comrades, crossing the short space between the two sides to rush the first barricade. Now the quarters were too close for archery to be effective, as the attackers took cover below the loopholes, and the barricade became a wall of clawing bodies and stabbing steel.

Conan crouched in the cover of an overturned cart. The planks shuddered as several bodies struck against it, straining to shove it aside. A face flashed across one of the openings through which the archers had shot. Conan jabbed clumsily with his broadsword, missed the throat and tore the point through the man's mouth. A spear thrust past the opening, as Conan lunged away. The man next to Conan caught the shaft and hauled inward. A fist clutched the haft, and, before the soldier could withdraw, Conan's blade severed wrist and spear together. Conan's companion fell away, still grasping the sundered spear. Conan glanced to see why the man did not return, and saw an arrow protruding from his face.

Another arrow bit into Conan's buckler. Korst had archers, too, and they were aiming at any opening in the barricade—seeking to pin down the defenders. More of the soldiers advanced behind makeshift mantlets, hurling themselves against the barricade. Swordblades, spears, and pole arms thrust and tore through the barrier from both sides, as the rebels fought to drive back the king's soldiers before they could dismantle this hastily thrown-up bulwark.

Axes thudded against timber. Conan waited until a plank was wrenched from the wagonbed, then thrust his swordpoint through the axe wielder's armpit. The broadsword was not suited for thrusting, but it worked well enough in a pinch, and the watered steel blade only rang from a counterstroke that would have snapped a lighter blade.

A halbard stabbed at him from an opening Conan had not seen appear. Its awl snagged his mail and crushed into the padded gambeson—inflicting no damage as Conan flung himself backward with the force of the blow. Carico's gift had saved his life. Conan did not waste his edge on the steel-guarded halbard shaft. Carico was a good smith, his political philosphies notwithstanding. Conan slammed the buckler behind the axe blade, lodged it there, hauled back sharply. The links in the mail were tight and solid, had held against the point of the awl when most mail would have parted. The halbard's owner was flung against the wagon-bed, as he sought to retain his grip on the haft. Conan's blade gutted him through the broken planks.

There were too many soldiers, Conan realized as the fight wore on. This barricade, quickly rebuilt after it had once before fallen, was being overwhelmed yet again. Korst's men had hit upon the tactic of typing ropes to portions of the barricade, dragging whole sections free—out of reach of the rebels' weapons. Conan knew they must fall back to the next barricade—and hope that it had been thrown together more substantially. It had been a mistake to keep the archers back, very probably; they might have picked men off the ropes. Conan made a mental note.

Just behind the barricade, a figure lurched from the doorway of a wineshop. Conan whirled to meet him, halted his sword stroke as he recognized Sifino's black-bearded face beneath a bloody bandage. Mordermi's lieutenant reeked of wine, and he stumbled from more than the blow to his skull. He blinked at Conan in some confusion.

"Crawled under the counter when the barricade fell," he muttered. "Must have passed out. Where's Carico? And how did we retake this barricade?"

"Carico's getting his leg patched up," Conan told him curtly. "Mordermi wants you. Take my horse and tell him our situation here. And tell him I'm going to have to fall

111

back to our second line. I need more men to hold."

To reinforce the urgency of his words, a large section of the barricade toppled outward. Conan shoved Sifino back into the doorway, as a massive ambry tumbled inward from the shifting pile. Almost instantly a pair of soldiers clambered into the breach. Conan cut down the first man, as Sifino brained the other with a table leg. Together they heaved the huge ambry back into the gap. Arrows thudded against its boards, as they rammed it into place.

Conan swore. "Can't hold this line. We'll burn it. That should give us time to regroup."

Sifino nodded, lurched back into the wineshop. He was back immediately with a half depleted wineskine and a full jar of lamp oil.

"This will set it burning right," he said, and began to slosh the oil onto the pile.

Conan flung a torch, and a splash of yellow flame licked across the tottering barricade. In a moment the wooden barrier was a mass of flame—driving attacker and defender back from the searing heat and suffocating smoke. A party of Zingaran soldiers, who had been tunneling beneath the barricade, rose up from the blazing pyre, danced crazily as the flames engulfed them.

Conan tore the wineskin from Sifino's grasp, drank greedily. "Tell Mordermi," he growled.

Carico joined him at the second barricade. The burly smith was reaccoutred and armed with a heavy double-bitted axe. His wounded leg was stiff beneath thick bandages, but nimble footwork was not required this day.

"Any news?" Conan asked grimly.

"We seem to be holding our own still." Carico gave his shoulder to the side of an ox cart, as Conan grasped a wheel. The stout wagonbed tilted, went over with a crash to fill the narrow gap in the barricade through which Conan's men had retreated. Heat from the blazing barrier they had quitted scorched their faces, as they shored the cart into position with heavy timbers.

"Korst's attack has bogged down," Carico continued. "It remains whether he'll keep on trying to force a major breakthrough, or launch an all-fronts assault down every airshaft and rathole that enters the Pits."

"Korst can't get in. We can't get out." Conan spat. "Well, he won't go away, and we can't keep retreating behind burning barricades."

"Our best hope is to fall back to where we can establish a stable line of defense," Carico said with optimism. "We've food and water enough to withstand a siege. Once the city sees that the free men of the Pit can stand firm against the tyrant's army, they'll rise against Rimanendo and we'll crush Korst's butchers in a vice."

"To our victory," Conan sourly toasted, and passed the wineskin to Carico. His own assessment of their situation was a gloomier one, but Carico's fervor was hard to resist. "When does our counterattack begin?"

"Santiddio is rallying the common folk of Kordava to our cause. Avvinti has taken a portion of our loot to tempt certain ambitious lords to lend us their support. All that remains is for the Pit to hold firm against Korst's army. Rimanendo rules through fear. When the people see that his power can be defied, then they will cease to fear—and remember only their hatred."

"What's this about Avvinti?" Conan blurted, not interested in Carico's oratory. "When did this happen? Mordermi couldn't have been fool enough to trust that silken jackanapes!"

"I'm no admirer of Avvinti," Carico put in, "but the man would never be a traitor to the White Rose. Avvinti has highborn friends and other such connections that make him invaluable to our cause. He left before dawn on a mission to ply the golden key, as they say."

"Before dawn?" Conan's suspicion only deepened. "Did Avvinti have wind of Korst's plans?"

"Oh, Korst's attack wasn't entirely unexpected," Carico reminded him. "Callidios predicted such a move, and it was obvious that we should lose no time in setting our plans in motion."

"But if Mordermi suspected that Korst would attack in force, why didn't we just take the loot and all of us clear out when Avvinti made his break?" Conan demanded. "Korst would have marched into the Pit without resistance, found we'd fled with the gold—and there'd have been no battle."

"No battle, no war." Carico explained the obvious. "We needed just this sort of bloody confrontation with Rimanendo's forces to solidify the people of Zingara behind our revolution."

Something in Conan's face warned him. Carico quickly amended: "All this is hindsight, of course. How could any of us have guessed that Korst would mount a full scale assault on the Pit?"

Conan remained silent, scowling moodily at the blazing wreckage of the outermost barricade. The draft had pulled most of the smoke outward, driving the king's soldiers back along Eel Street and out of the Pit. The interlude in the fighting had given the defenders time to draw breath and shore up their fortifications. It also gave Conan time to wonder whether his friends were fools or madmen.

Sifino returned before the blaze had entirely subsided.

"What did Mordermi say?" Conan asked him.

"Couldn't talk to Mordermi," Sifino swore. "He and that damn Stygian are in deep dark council—just the two of them—and they were not to be disturbed. I didn't wait around. Left word with Sandokazi, and beat it back here with all the men I could find."

"Callidios?" Conan's scowl deepened. "Crom's devils!

114

Has Mordermi gone mad, too! The time is past for hatching plots and crazy schemes. We've got to *fight* if we're going to stay alive!''

He came to a decision. ''Sifino, you take over here again. I'm going to find out how the other barricades are holding out. Then I'll report to Mordermi—and if he's too busy scheming with Callidios to fight a battle, I'll lead us myself if I have to!''

The Pit was a maze of twisted passageways and cellars beneath cellars. While its peculiar architecture made any forthright assault impossible, by the same token it was virtually impossible to present a stable line of defense within its labyrinth. Contemptuous of the Pit's capability to repel an organized assault, Korst had so far elected to hold to his original battle strategy—to overrun the defenders with a massive, decisive breakthrough on any of three fronts. But Conan realized that, should they continue to frustrate Korst's advance, the king's general would retaliate with a mass assault down every stairway and crevice that gave access into the Pit. Initial casualties would be enormous, and his forces would be spread out across the entire district—but the Pit must inevitably be overwhelmed by the superior forces of the Royal Zingaran Army.

This awareness made the Cimmerian reckless. Unless the barricades held, the Pit would fall; if the barricades held, the Pit would fall. Only if an outside force broke the siege could the Pit be saved. Conan held little hope for Santiddio's attempt to rally the citizens of Kordava to the doomed cause of its slum world, and he was confident that Avvinti was well on his way to Aquilonia by now with the fortune his former comrades had died to win. It was only a matter of waiting until Korst's impatience overruled his taste for military precision.

Conan rode into Water Street and found the barricades there all but abandoned. Fires had spread throughout the

115

dingy waterfront section, and both sides had been forced to flee as the holocaust engulfed the border of the Pit and fanned outward into Kordava proper.

At Old Market Street the defenders had underminded the columns that supported the street and buildings overhead. The resulting cave-in had killed as many rebels as soldiers, but Old Market Street was buried beneath a mountain of rubble. Korst would need a month to dig through here.

Conan made a hasty circuit of the Pit, ruthlessly forcing his mount through the aimlessly milling crowds. Everywhere there were barricades—sealing off the inconsequential passages and alleys that gave access to the buried city. Windows were boarded, doors barred. Anxious faces glared from behind cover, waiting for the enemy to attack. No soldiers were in evidence. Korst would hardly have abandoned his assault. With a sense of foreboding, Conan jabbed his heels to his horse and galloped back toward Eel Street.

Panic-stricken fugitives alerted him for what awaited him there.

Conan urged his mount onward against the rush of the mob. Turning onto Eel Street he took in the disaster at a glance.

Korst had concentrated his attack here, as the other advances failed. As his soldiers stormed the barricade, a squad of Korst's Strikers stealthily descended into a bordello that fronted on Eel Street behind the bulwark there, slaughtering any they found within. In the fury of combat at the barricade, their presence there was unsuspected—until the invaders burst out in force to strike the rebel defenders from behind. In the melee, exact numbers were impossible to guess. Fearing that a major breakthrough had taken place, the reserve force that Conan had left to erect a third barricade deserted their position and fled.

Conan charged into their midst, laying about him with the flat of his sword. "Stand and fight, you pukeblooded

116

cowards!'' he roared. ''Where will you hide? Stand and fight—or die!''

Despite their panic, the Cimmerian's presence overawed them. For a moment there was hesitation.

''Follow me, you gutless dogs!'' Conan railed at them. ''Back to the barricades! We can hold Korst's butchers! He's been driven back from every other front! Stand and fight, I tell you! Let them overrun us here, and we're all of us dead men! Follow me!''

Without looking back to see if they obeyed him, Conan rode through them—intending to fight alone to the death rather than die with cowards. Some few shuffled shame-facedly away, but the main part of the mob turned and followed the giant Cimmerian.

Clearing the gap in the partially completed third barricade, Conan rode down two of Korst's Strikers before they knew their death was upon them. In the cramped quarters there was no room to maneuver—neither was there space to dodge the flailing hooves and Conan's slashing blade. Soldiers spun about to face this new peril—giving respite to those rebels who were trapped against the second barricade. With a roar, those who had followed Conan's one-man charge poured into the fray.

His horse screamed and stumbled—hamstrung. Conan vaulted clear of the saddle as the beast fell—its thrashing hooves and crushing weight killing several of those who could not leap back in time. Conan rolled to his knees, stunned for an instant by the impact with the street. A sword slashed downward. Conan clumsily parried, all but lost his grip on the basket hilt. His assailant grinned; a double-bitted axe split his face in a far wider grin.

Carico grasped his shoulder and hauled the Cimmerian to his feet. ''Well done, lad!'' he applauded. ''Next time you've a notion to sell your sword to some great lord, enlist in his cavalry and not the infantry.''

Conan saved his breath to cut the legs out from under a soldier who vaulted over the crumbling barricade. More of Korst's Strikers were darting out from the bordello, engaging the rebels who had followed Conan. The barricade was disintegrating before his eyes.

"Fall back!" Conan yelled. "Let's set this ablaze!"

"No time!" Carico groaned. A section gave inward as he spoke.

Attacking in full strength, Korst's men had used the diversion to smash through the barrier behind an improvised mantlet. Zingaran archers left fly from behind cover, as their comrades poured through the breach.

"Fall back!" Conan commanded. An arrow skidded from his burgonet. "Fall back!" His command made a strategic retreat out of a rout. "Take up positions at the third barricade!"

"And when that falls?" Carico muttered. The battle now seemed somewhat less the political exercise.

"We'll raise another barricade and fall back to it," Conan laughed harshly. "We're going to crush Korst in a vice—remember?"

XI. The Final Guard Marches

Along Kordava's waterfront, smoke and flame raised a lurid banner above the hell of carnage that raged within the Pit.

Beneath the leaden waters of the bay, a horror far greater emerged implacably into the flame-lit twilight.

There were none to witness its coming. At first. The harbor was ablaze to the water's edge; Korst's soldiers had abandoned their cordon here, had fled from the intense heat along with those whose shops and dwellings were being consumed. Elsewhere, the riot of battle and the swarming ranks of burgundy and gold clad soldiers drove the curious and the morbid back to the safety of their homes. In a fight such as this, any man not in the king's livery was a potential enemy, and Korst's men weren't known for their restraint.

Had any watcher been standing upon the deserted quay, he might have noticed a sudden turmoil beneath the oily waves that surged against the stone steps that led down from the sea wall to the beach. Another glance, and he would have been startled to see a row of swimmers' heads breaking the surface—their faces uncanny in the reflected glow of the flames. A moment later, and another row of faces would break water, as the first line thrust shoulders and chests out of the sea. Not swimmers; they were walking upon the sea bottom, striding up out of the waves.

The first of them gained the submerged row of steps and marched upward in close file. Behind them, a steady procession of silent figures continued to trudge forward from out of the troubled sea. They uttered no sounds—only the rattle of their accoutrements and the unnaturally loud tread of their sandaled feet broke the silence. In the fiery dusk, accoutrements and flesh alike seemed imbued with a dark, glossy sheen, like polished obsidian or jet. Water slid from their skin and clothing as if from waxed glass, leaving them dry and gleaming as they strode forward from the stairway to form ranks upon the quay.

Their every movement bespoke well-drilled precision, as if an elite regiment were forming for parade. Absent was the clash of steel; instead there crept sounds that were somehow like the slither of a whetted knife on oiled stone, or the shiver of icicles strummed by an arctic wind, or the scrape of nails upon dry slate, or the death-scream of shattered crystal. The flames picked out crimson stars upon spikes of maces, edges of swords, bits of war axes—and here, too, all was black and shining and sharp as broken glass.

As if obedient to silent command, the first group to form up marched forward from the quay and into the flame-lit streets. Behind them, a second group took their position; and behind them, a continuous file of obsidian warriors emerged from the sea and onto the quay. And like the waves of the sea, they came forth upon the shore in tireless, numberless measure.

The holocaust that had driven Korst's soldiers back from their attack along Water Street (so called because an occasional spring tide flooded it) threatened to raze this squalid section of Kordava's waterfront. There were some few who scurried desperately about the edges of the blaze, seeking to salvage whatever they might from the conflagration.

These were the first to look upon the coming of the Final Guard. They fled.

Their reaction was understandable. The fire had leaped across two decrepit storehouses that shouldered the street that led down to the quay. Portions of wall had toppled into the street, and explosive gouts of intense flame rolled like molten thunderheads between the two blazing structures. Through this firestorm marched the first hundred of the Final Guard, as heedless as if they strode past blowing leaves.

Beyond the flames, the army's cordon still maintained a patient watch for fugitives from below—a circle of cats waiting to pounce. At the sound of frightened shouts, they turned to see the century of warriors impassively advancing through a wall of fire. Some fled. The others died.

With the breakthrough along Eel Street imminent, Korst had brought up the main body of his troops to this sector. Despite earlier setbacks and heavy losses from the unexpected resistance, the action promised to conclude to the general's satisfaction. He had drawn the rebels to pitched battle, and now he would crush them in one decisive engagement. Some might flee—to be hunted down in the aftermath—but the abortive revolution would be smashed, annihilated root and branch. Rimanendo would be generous with the general whose victory avenged the king's honor and by the same stroke destroyed those who threatened his rule.

Their weapons crimson now with bright blood, the Final Guard advanced upon Eel Street.

Their brief, deadly skirmish with the cordon had already alerted the main body of Korst's soldiers to the presence of the Final Guard. A few survivors had blurted out garbled reports too fantastic to be regarded as anything more than panic-stricken delusion. Expecting no more than a desperate sortie by the beleaguered rebels, the Royal Zingaran Army marched quickly to contain their counterattack. In the gathering darkness beyond the flames, they may not immediately have remarked upon the unnatural appearance of their foe — perhaps assuming that the rebels had smeared themselves with some black pigment as a stratagem for night combat.

A shower of arrows greeted the silent warriors as they emerged through the smoke-filled gloom. They neither sought cover, nor did their line falter. Korst's archers passed it off to poor light and good armor, and stepped back to let the infantry deal with the rebel sortie.

Their battle cries strangely shrill without an answering roar from their impassive foemen, the Zingaran soldiers hurled themselves upon the Final Guard. It was as if an immense wave had thundered against a basalt cliff. The wave broke apart in a surging explosion of spray. This spray was red.

Weapons of steel shattered against adamantine flesh. Blades that shimmered like black diamond ripped through mail and flesh and bone as if it were one. Korst's soldiers were literally torn apart. War cries became death shrieks, blunted by the sickening soft chopping sound of sundered flesh, the pattering plash of blood, the dull fall of dismembered limbs.

Elder sorcery had transmuted human warriors into indestructible killing machines. Creatures of living stone, the Final Guard moved with all the speed and reflexes of the master warriors they once had been. But now their invulnerable bodies were driven by muscles of supernatural strength. Diamond-hard weapons ripped and smashed through armor and flesh; obsidian fists closed upon human limbs, tearing muscle and sinew from crushed bone.

The horror was so intense that those who witnessed it seemed momentarily paralyzed. Then, as the front ranks were butchered without mercy, their comrades who followed

122

them shook off the numbness of shock and turned in panic. The soldiers to the rear, still unaware of the doom that marched toward them, heard the cries and—assuming only that the front ranks had met unexpected rebel resistance— came forward in double time to aid them. They collided with those who sought to flee. Officers shouted orders; panic-stricken soldiers yelled incoherently, gibbered mindless answers to questions. Confined by the narrow street, front and rear ranks locked together in a tangled mass of immobility.

Into the milling chaos, the Final Guard marched forward—swinging their blood-drenched weapons with all the tireless precision of harvestmen reaping with scythes. It was a red harvest. The street ran with human gore; crushed bodies buried the pavement. Creatures of stone, the Final Guard bore the ponderous mass of living statues. As they had earlier marched across the bottom of the sea, so now they waded into a human sea. Their tread struck the paving with the heavy impact of a draft horse's hooves. Those who stumbled in the press were crushed beneath their feet; others, unable to flee, were smashed against the wall by the relentless advance of the Final Guard.

Writhing back upon itself like the coils of a wounded python, the Royal Zingaran Army halted its advance, turned about in a broken rout. It left a trail of crushed red things behind it, and, marching upon the trail as if on parade, century after century of the Final Guard, marching out of the sea and out of the abyss of time.

XII. To Follow the Road of Kings

At the third barricade, Conan fought on with the ferocity of a wounded lion. The scales of battle had tipped against the rebels; defeat was certain, escape improbable. The soldiers had driven past the barricade in a human avalanche, forcing the rebels back to their last line of defense. Sifino had gone down somewhere in their retreat; Carico, his wounded thigh bleeding again, swung his great axe with faltering strength. Most of the defenders were slain; some few had fought clear of the melee and fled. Leading those who remained in a final stand, Conan fought savagely to throw back the Zingaran advance—dealing death all about him without a thought for his own hide. They might kill him, but Conan vowed they would not again make him a prisoner. When he fell, those who saw would know by the dead piled about him that a Cimmerian did not sell his life cheaply.

Flung up in a frantic effort, the third barricade was too flimsy to withstand their rush for long. Already Korst's soldiers hurtled through ragged gaps in the bulwark. If anything, their very numbers held them back as much as the failing rebel defense—so many attackers had swarmed into Eel Street that by now they were too crowded together to fight as effectively. But the fighting would soon be over.

At the uproar behind him, Conan at first thought Korst's soldiers had again outflanked their line of defense and had come upon the rebels from behind. But as cheers and glad shouts echoed from the rear, Conan risked a glance to learn the cause.

Mordermi, rapier brandished gallantly in his good hand, left shoulder impressively bandaged, rode at the head of his men. Fresh defenders rushed to relieve the exhausted handful who still held the barricade. The outlaw leader had committed his reserve—and to judge from the excited mob who surged behind him, Mordermi must have rallied those who had manned the barricades elsewhere.

Letting other bodies take his place in the thick of the fighting, Conan greeted his friend with a bloody handclasp. "You're as pretty as a king's victory monument," Conan grinned wearily. "But you may have waited too late. Korst has too many men; he's cut into us too far."

"Mitra, you northern barbarians are a gloomy lot!" Mordermi laughed, sheathing his sword to embrace the Cimmerian's shoulders. "Korst is in a trap, not us. The cat has crept too far into the rathole! In a moment you'll see."

Conan remembered Carico's specious talk of the city taking arms for the rebel cause. "Then Santiddio . . . ?"

"Not Santiddio," Mordermi informed him. "Callidios."

"What can that lotus-dreamer . . . !"

"You saw," Mordermi said in a tone of reproof. "Sandokazi verified his words. The Final Guard."

"Stone devils that guard their king's bones at the bottom of the sea!"

"Not any longer. Callidios has summoned them forth."

"How can that Stygian renegade command such demons!"

"Well, Conan," said Mordermi, "if I knew that, then I wouldn't need Callidios, would I?"

"You mean you've let yourself get sucked in by that madman's lies!"

"Look," Mordermi pointed.

Conan stared.

It was difficult to discern much of what was taking place beyond the barricade. Thick smoke obscured what little light there was, and the barricade itself blocked out most of the street beyond. It was the sudden shift in the spirit of the attackers that Conan felt. A moment ago their cries had been imbued with the jubilation of impending triumph. Now there was a distinct note of fear. The arrival of Mordermi's reinforcements could not have inspired this abrupt sense of terror.

For a macabre interval of time, the battle shuddered to a halt. Both sides sensed the chill breath of alien horror. Men in the fury of combat virtually froze in midstride; weapons that were slashing for an enemy's flesh drifted to a halt as if the air had turned to glass and imprisoned them. Conan, who had seen men locked in combat roll from atop a city wall and never pause in their struggle until they smashed to the earth, could not credit his eyes now. Truly sorcery had cast its foul shadow upon this field of battle, and although its spell might have swung the scythe of defeat from his comrades to their enemy, Conan suddenly knew in his heart that he should never have returned to Kordava with Callidios undrowned.

The screams began.

At first the soldiers who paused before the barricade sought to turn from the attack to discover what manner of disaster had struck those to the rear. Panic claimed the attackers, as they struggled to retreat along Eel Street. Then they knew what terror had engendered such cries from veteran warriors—and with that came the knowledge that retreat was impossible.

The Final Guard marched into Eel Street.

In another moment, the soldiers were fleeing back toward the barricade, seeking only to escape the inhuman warriors who stalked them. They rushed the barricade in blind panic. Fear made them heedless of the defenders there. They almost carried the barricade now in their panic, for even the bravest warrior has the instinct of self-preservation in combat, and does not witlessly fling himself upon the blades of his foemen, as these soldiers did now.

Conan, who had looked upon massacre from both sides, turned away from the slaughter in disgust. To kill an enemy who has lost his will to defend himself was not the way Cimmerians made war.

"Stop them!" he growled to Mordermi.

"Don't worry," Mordermi misread his meaning. "Callidios can control them."

"I mean, stop this butchery! Let Korst's men surrender."

"My people need a victory," Mordermi shrugged. "And we've suffered much from Rimanendo's dogs."

Conan swore, but by now the issue was past. No more of the soldiers struggled across the barricade. Along Eel Street resounded the heavy stamp of marching feet, muffled suggestively to the barely audible snap of crushed bone. Out of the darkness, the ebony ranks of the Final Guard lumbered into view.

They halted before the barricade—at attention, awaiting further commands. The rebels paused in the flush of their victory to gape anxiously upon their demonic allies. Jubilant shouts died into whispers of fear.

Mordermi took charge of the situation.

"Look upon them, my friends!" he shouted, riding forward unafraid. "These are the allies who have been summoned to bring victory to our cause. With the assistance of my valued friend and counselor, the noted wizard Callidios, I have brought forth from the age of legends an army of indestructible warriors. You have seen for yourselves how such warriors can aid us. Salute them now, my friends—our allies in our war of liberation, the Final Guard!"

The cheers were ragged at first. Then, perhaps in reaction to earlier fear, swelled into a deafening ovation.

Mordermi let it build to a pitch, then raised his arm for silence.

"General Korst has fled with his pack of killers to the kennel of his master. Even now Rimanendo quakes in his ermine robes as he learns of our victory, and he prays that his soldiers and his palace walls may protect him from the wrath of the people he has misruled. But tell me, my friends. Can his soldiers and his walls protect the tyrant from the justice of the people!"

Mordermi waited as the chorus of *NO!* reached a crescendo.

"Then take arms now, my friends! With our invincible allies before us, we march to depose a depraved tyrant and his corrupt court! The hour of our liberation is at hand!"

The wild march through the streets of Kordava that followed upon Mordermi's harangue, for all the heady emotion and excitement of the moment, never quite lost the quality of a nightmare to Conan.

They streamed up out of the Pit, the despised and downtrodden citizens of the shadow world—their numbers swelling with each step of the way. Carico, too lame to walk, yielded to his pride and Conan's urging and rode astride a horse—after making Conan promise to ride beside him to catch him if he fell off. As they moved through the city, Santiddio actually led a crowd of several thousand, marching behind the banner of the White Rose. Conan wondered how many had rallied to Santiddio's people's army before news of the Pit's victory spread throughout Kordava. Santiddio greeted them boisterously—out of character for him—and he and Carico consoled one another that Avvinti was not here to share the hour. Mordermi—accompanied by San-dokazi until her brother joined them—rode on ahead of the steadily growing procession.

Of Callidios there was no sign, but his presence was felt beyond doubt. The Final Guard, one thousand silent demons of death, marched before the rebel throng.

They moved through Kordava at will, meeting no resis-tance. Men and women either ran out to join their ranks, or remained discreetly behind locked doors as the banner of the White Rose streamed past. General Korst, disengaging from the impossible combat with the Final Guard, had fled the massacre of the Pit with as many men as he could save. Behind the fortress walls of Rimanendo's palace Korst sought to regroup his men for a stand against the rebels and their inhuman allies. But the disaster at the Pit had been too demoralizing for the king's army. Fugitives from the massacre had carried tales of their comrades that all too convincingly relayed the horror of that slaughter. To stand against a human opponent was one matter; to face the un-stoppable forces of black sorcery quite another. The Royal Zingaran Army deserted in entire companies of officers and men.

King Rimanendo had ruled too long as a corrupt and hated tyrant. The Zingarans had endured his reign not from loyalty to their monarch, but out of fear. Now the heroes of the White Rose had brought forth a power greater than Rimanendo's army. It was the despot's time to know fear—a time his rebellious subjects intended to make mercifully brief. Deserted by all those who had the chance and wit to flee, King Rimanendo cowered in his opulent chambers, while the last of his faithful dogs prepared a hopeless de-fense.

Their march upon Rimanendo's palace was unchecked. Only as they approached the fortress barracks was there any show of armed resistance, and this from a small garrison who either had not heard or did not believe the lurid tales of the rebels' demon army. The front ranks of the Final Guard mowed the garrison down almost without breaking stride; the soldiers might as well have tried to check an avalanche by fending it off barehanded. The short, bloody spectacle only inflamed the mob all the more—as those who had not seen before now witnessed the awesome destructive power of the Final Guard.

Conan remembered the massacre of the Gundermen at Venarium, in which he had taken part several years before. The Cimmerian clans had united to annihilate this fort town that the Aquilonians built to colonize the southern marches of Cimmeria. Men, women and children were butchered; Venarium burned to the ground. For Conan it was a glorious memory. The massacre he now participated in would remain forever in his memory as well, but Conan knew he would never glory in its remembrance.

The wall that encircled the royal palace displayed a steel crown of weapons and armor, scintillant in the torchlight and the sullen glow of the distant conflagration that yet ravened the waterfront. The stars were blinded by a veil of smoke.

Perhaps the fortress walls gave them confidence. Whatever the case, it was evident that General Korst had no thoughts of surrendering the palace to the rabble. From atop the walls, iron-barbed arrows streaked downward into the mob. Behind the battlements, petraries flung a hail of stones full into the advancing throng. Men and women howled in agony and rage, as death swept the rebel horde—suddenly reminding them that Mordermi was leading them to battle, not in a holiday procession. Recoiling from the deadly barrage of arrows and stones, the rebels sought the cover of adjacent buildings.

Conan backed his mount into the cover of a buttress, watched to see what effect stone missiles would have against the Final Guard. The petraries hurled missiles ranging from baskets of rocks the size of a man's fist to single stones of fifty to sixty pounds. The smaller stones pelted the Final Guard with no more effect than a barrage of snowballs. An instant later a small boulder smashed full into the breast and shoulders of one of the guardsmen—toppling the stone devil to the ground under its impact. The missile broke into shards, bounding away; the warrior of living stone picked himself up, unscathed. Its movement was so natural that Conan would not have been surprised to see it dust the rock dust from its jet breastplate.

But impervious to arrows and stones or not, the Final Guard did not stand idle in the face of the barrage. As the soldiers let fly to repel the army of rabble, the Final Guard formed a close column and marched swiftly toward the fortress' main gate. From the barbican, the hail of missiles intensified—outlined now against the night as vats of flaming oil streamed down upon the attacking demons. The defenders might have poured scented bath water, for all the damage their frantic efforts inflicted upon the silent ranks.

The Final Guard reached the massive gate of the fortress—sturdy timbers braced with thick bars of iron, built to withstand the crushing impacts of a battering ram. The onlookers from both sides of the wall caught their breath and waited.

Sheathing their weapons for a moment, the front ranks of the Final Guard pressed their hands to the stout oaken barrier. For a heartbeat, thews of living stone strained against the handiwork of man. Only for an instant was their advance checked. Then, in a death groan of bending iron bolts and splintering oaken timbers, the fortress gate caved inward. A broken, sagging thing, the gate crashed down upon the defenders who had desperately thrown their shoulders to the creaking portal. Past its splintered wreckage, the Final Guard entered the fortress—dealing death to those whose faith in fortress walls and human weapons was now betrayed.

For only a moment did the crowd hold back in awe. Then, with a hungry roar from ten thousand throats, the people of Kordava rushed into the doomed palace to seek vengeance upon their hated oppressors. The beast was down. Now the pack closed for the kill.

Conan, determined to be in on the finish as well, nudged his mount forward. It was only a short time ago, he reflected, that he had fully expected to lie dead in the blood and filth of the Pit. Now he went to loot a king's palace.

With the Final Guard striking down all those who stood in their path, the assault on Rimanendo's fortress had passed the stage of battle and become sheer butchery. There was no quarter from the Final Guard. Those soldiers and retainers who attempted to surrender to Mordermi were pulled to pieces by the mob. Some escaped by shedding their burgundy and gold livery and joining the bloodthirsty crowds; others managed to take advantage of the chaos to get over the wall and flee beyond the reach of the rabble. And some, disdaining flight, rallied together for a final stand—preserving honor if not their lives.

Conan found where General Korst had fallen, with the last of his dreaded Strikers in a hopeless defense of the palace entrance. The mob had passed over their corpses—seeking richer loot for the moment. Conan paused there, respectful of a brave soldier who had served his king to the death.

The blue-black beard was clotted with dark blood, his chest shattered by the crushing blow of a mace, but not all the life had drained from him yet. Korst opened his eyes, returned Conan's gaze, and recognition showed through the weary pain.

"I know you," Korst said dully. "The Cimmerian mutineer. You escaped the gallows. Mordermi made you his right-hand man."

"I offered you my sword," Conan's tone held rancour

still. "You repaid me with a hempen noose. I'll follow my fortune with Mordermi instead."

Korst's eyes looked past Conan. "So once did I follow my fortune. It led me to this. Look upon me, Cimmerian. It may be that you look upon your future self."

Conan started to retort, then saw that Korst would not hear him.

Pushing throught the throngs of looters who had overrun the royal palace in every room, Conan went looking for Mordermi. He found the victorious outlaw leader battering down the heavy door that gave entrance to Rimanendo's private chambers. Conan lent his strength to the broken column they had seized for a ram, and the door burst asunder.

Conan was not prepared for the scene that awaited them within.

Frightened out of his drink-clouded wits, King Rimanendo had barricaded himself in his chambers with sycophants and catamites to console him in his terror. These, knowing that Rimanendo's rule was at an end, had determined to win the favor of Kordava's new masters by turning upon the fallen monarch.

When Mordermi and Conan strode across the threshold of the king's chambers, two youths minced toward them from the huddled group within. Their hair was curled and scented, their bare flesh oiled and rouged, and they carried between them a golden tray. Upon the tray was a golden crown, and the crown still rested upon the severed head of Rimanendo.

XIII. A New Order and a Coronation

It was decided that Mordermi should be king.

Initially Mordermi would not hear of it, but they argued down his objections.

Rimanendo and his court had perished in the palace massacre. The king had left neither issue nor heir, nor was it likely that the rebels would have surrendered Kordava to any of the tyrant's blood. Nor, with the Final Guard at their command, was it likely that any claimant to the throne could have demanded the crown from the victorious rebels.

The old age of corrupt despotism was past. A new order now ruled in Kordava, and from Kordava claimed to rule all of Zingara.

This was not simply a change of rulers, Santiddio liked to point out, as when a palace revolt or *coup d'état* does no more than exchange one set of scoundrels for another. Rather, the victory of the White Rose marked the beginning of a new social order for Zingara. The White Rose would draw up a new constitution for the people of Zingara—giving the people a voice in their governing, implementing new laws that would insure equal justice for all the people.

Clearly, so radical and important an undertaking would require a great deal of time and deliberation to bring about.

Committees must be formed, representatives elected, ideas and facts must be compiled, studied, discussed. In the interim, a revolutionary committee of the White Rose should undertake the management of Zingara's government.

Moreover, these were perilous times for the new order. True, the Final Guard secured the freedom of Kordava from antirevolutionary forces, but Zingara was a large country, threatened by enemies from within who wanted a return to the old despotism of their class, from without by enemies who saw the success of the new order as a danger to their own corrupt rule. From the revolutionary committee, consequently, one member should be chosen who should have dictatorial powers with which to deal with any threat to the new order. Such a man, moreover, should be a leader of proven ability, a man of the people himself, and yet a man who could lead the people to victory in battle. Such powers would be only temporary, of course, pending the finalization of a new constitution and elected representatives.

While it was undeniably true, Mordermi was forced to admit, that the situation called for emergency measures, and that he did indeed conform to these qualifications; nonetheless, to accept the crown of Zingara when the king he had defeated was barely cold meat . . .

Avvinti, returning from his mission—whose success had been assured once news of the rebel victory reached the outlying gentry—made the telling point that, in a period of transition from one mode of government to another, the Zingaran aristocracy, whose support was essential to their fledgling rule, would feel far more at ease pledging their loyalty to a king, with all the sanctity and tradition of the kingship, than to some committee president.

Mordermi protested. In the end he conceded to their logic.

It never failed to amaze Conan that his friends could exhaust themselves with so much verbiage and tortuous argument before agreeing upon the obvious. He put it down as another of the incomprehensible rituals that preoccupied civilized folk.

And through such rituals was the provisional government of Zingara established. Mordermi was to be king. As leaders of the major factions of the White Rose, the triumvirate of Avvinti, Santiddio, and Carico would head the revolutionary committee. Callidios, whose political acumen had proven to be no less brilliant than his command of sorcerous arts, would serve as prime minister. Conan, whose bravery and prowess in battle had made him a popular hero, would become general of the Zingaran Revolutionary Army.

"From common mercenary to general of the king's army in a matter of months is some promotion," Conan observed at Mordermi's coronation.

"Well yes, it is quick work, isn't it?" Mordermi laughed, motioning to a servant to bring them more wine. "But no more so than rising from prince of thieves to king of Zingara!"

He laughed some more at his own wit. "Besides," Mordermi went on, more serious now. "I need a friend I can trust as my general. You're young, Conan, but you've seen more fighting than most veterans—certainly you know more of battles than any of my band of rogues or Santiddio's circle of high-minded fops. And I dare not entrust my army to any of Korst's old officers, or to any of Avvinti's friends among the great lords. You're my friend, Conan—and the only friend I know I can trust."

"If that is so, then heed my counsel," Conan said earnestly. "Get rid of Callidios."

"Cimmerians aren't ones to sway from an idea, I can see. I need Callidios. It will take weeks to regroup the army. Until then, we'd be easy prey for any of the great lords with a private army and any scab of royal blood, if we didn't have the Final Guard as a weapon in our defense. Callidios knows the secret of their command. I don't."

"Give me time to build this Zingaran Revolutionary Army into something more than one of Santiddio's slogans," Conan promised, "and you'll have no need for any army of stone devils."

"Come to me then with your counsel," Mordermi suggested.

"What? Are you two the only sober ones here?" Santiddio lurched toward them, steadying himself not too well on his sister's shoulder. "A plague on your new crown, Mordermi, if it's kept you sober at your own coronation."

"Conan and I are discussing the new army. Show more respect when you address the king and his general."

Santiddio made a belch that did credit to so thin a man. "Avvinti thinks it would be politic for you to share some of your presence with Baron Manovra and Count Perizi, who have come to the coronation of their new king."

"Of course." Mordermi bowed to Sandokazi. "Your arm, milady? You'll dazzle their shrewd brains with your beauty, and I'll get them to promise to any alliance."

Conan watched the three of them walk across the crowded ballroom, thinking back on their first meeting. Mordermi made a truly majestic figure in his court attire and golden crown. Santiddio still looked like a drunken student, decked out in his best suit of clothes. Sandokazi was radiant in a shoulderless gown of stiff brocade, swelling in many petticoats from the tightly corsetted waist. Conan, glancing down at his own none-too-fresh garments, wondered whether the king's general was expected to dress formally for the coronation.

Rimanendo's palace—Mordermi's now—had been made presentable to some extent following the night of looting short days before. At some point it must have occurred to Mordermi that he and his men were plundering his own future palace. The people of Kordava had hailed Mordermi

138

as their new king amidst loud cheers and wild celebration—
the outlaw leader had always been a hero to them, and as
the leader of the victorious rebels he was liberator as well
as dashing rogue.

"Let the people proclaim me their king," Mordermi said.
"That will be coronation enough."

Avvinti, reminding him that Zingara's gentry must recognize him as their king also, pointed out that form must be
observed.

So it was. In the half-demolished palace that he had taken
through force, Mordermi was crowned king of Zingara,
according to the hallowed rituals of the aristocratic realm.
As if to compensate, Mordermi invited all of Kordava to
his coronation. The courtyard where a short time before
bodies and wreckage covered the flagstones once again
seethed with a riotous mob, although these had come to
revel and it was wine that flowed so freely on this day.

Conan drained his goblet, wondering that he did not share
in their spirit of headlong gaiety. His friends had won a
tremendous victory, he had been rewarded with high position. When he wandered south to seek his fortune among
the civilized nations, this day would have then seemed to
him a mad dream.

Korst's dying face would not stay out of his thoughts.
His final words mocked him now. Had Korst only voiced
his bitterness over his fate, or in death was the man fey?
Conan had seen this occur with men and women of his own
race when death was near.

Conan spat, glared at the richly dressed worthies who
crowded the ballroom. Outside, clamoring in the courtyard
and spilling their drunken revel into the surrounding streets,
these were his sort of people. With them he could get drunk
and forget the mockery in a dying man's eyes. He'd find a
merry wench who was forward with her favors, and if there

were those who wanted to sing or to brawl, he was ready to join in with either.

Conan stalked from the ballroom in distaste. Crom! The crown was not yet warm on Mordermi's brow, and already the place was turning into a royal court!

XIV. Conan Takes the Field

The weeks that followed were ones of tremendous activity for Conan. Time and again the Cimmerian cursed himself for accepting this task. While this high position was indeed a great honor, Conan quickly learned that generals had more duties to perform than merely to fight battles, and that his prowess as a warrior was only one of the qualifications necessary in his new role. Conan was disgruntled to find himself reviewing troops when he might otherwise have been dicing with other off-duty footsoldiers in the barracks, puzzling over lists and reports late at night when he should be drinking and wenching in Kordava's taverns, or trying patiently to sort out the protests and arguments of his officers when his first impulse was to crack a few skulls.

But Mordermi was depending on him to see it through, so Conan gritted his teeth and got the job done.

While Conan would not admit it, the presence of the Final Guard made his task possible. In the first weeks of Mordermi's reign, while Conan struggled to weld together a new army from the aftermath of the rebels' victory, it was doubtful that the fledgling Zingaran Revolutionary Army could have defended Kordava from any major assault. Certain of the great lords with their private armies murmured that it was intolerable to permit the throne of Zingara to be usurped by a common outlaw, while the kings of the other Hyborian nations pondered the fact that an expeditionary force might well place their puppet upon the throne of strife-torn Zingara.

But the reports of the violent overthrow of King Rimanendo's reign did not stint on lurid details of the carnage wrought by the Final Guard. Kordava was defended by an army of indestructible stone warriors. It was never wise to attack openly any ruler who was served by the powers of dark sorcery; the prudent course was to wait until some hidden weakness could be found. And while the jackals crouched and waited, Mordermi moved swiftly to establish his rule.

Conan's dilemma was an unusual one for a victorious faction; the victors had no army. The rebel force had been a coalition of Mordermi's outlaw band and the White Rose—neither of these an army by any stretch of the word—whose ranks had been filled by armed citizens during the course of the battle. The battle in the Pit had cost the lives of many of the rebels from the original core of fighters, and those who came forward now to join the victorious revolutionaries were for the most part lacking in military training or combat experience.

"Their only worth is as bodies to fill the ranks," Conan fumed. "An enemy might mistake them for soldiers and strike at them instead of someone who knows which end of his helmet to poke his head through. They might be good in a street brawl, but I could no more lead them into the field than I can forge a sword by sticking nails together with spit."

"Well, what do you need?" Mordermi asked.

"I need real soldiers. Declare an amnesty for all of the Royal Zingaran Army who'll swear allegiance to you. I know most of the mercenary commanders. They scattered during the massacre, but I can bring them back with a

142

promise of amnesty and enough gold.''

"Gold is no problem. Can we count on their loyalty?"

"The mercenaries will sell their swords to any ruler who can pay. As for the Royal Army, most of those who were loyal to Rimanendo died with Korst in the final battle. If Rimanendo had been well loved or had left an heir it might be different, but as things stand they'll take amnesty and be glad for a chance to throw their lot in with the new regime.''

"It might be wise to accept the offer of some of Avvinti's friends who have volunteered officers and companies from their personal armies to bolster our forces.''

"I thought you didn't trust Avvinti," Conan reminded him.

"I don't," Mordermi said blandly. "But I don't trust Carico either, with his crackbrained politics—and I've noticed that far too many of his followers have rushed to enlist in my army.''

Conan decided he had far too many other problems on his hands to concern himself with his friends' obsession with such bickering and hair-splitting. His task was to build the Zingaran Revolutionary Army into something that might conceivably have need of a general. And in this the Cimmerian was successful. The amnesty brought a great many recruits out of hiding; Mordermi's gold lured a great many more. Conan managed to assemble a corps of officers with the experience and ability to take charge of the bulk of the organizational drudgery, eventually learned to delegate responsibility—a difficult adjustment for the Cimmerian, who was a loner, and consequently reluctant to entrust others with key matters.

Gold, as Mordermi had stated, was no problem to the new reign. The plunder of Rimanendo's court had made the spoils of their raid on the late king's pleasure palace seem no more than the handful of brass coins in a beggar's bowl.

And this in turn dwindled to insignificance beside the loot of Kalenius' tomb.

Since summoning forth the Final Guard, Callidios was not often to be seen. Whether the Stygian renegade was delving ever deeper into the paths he followed, or merely staying lost in the fumes of the yellow lotus, Conan wasn't certain. He suspected the latter, hoped such was the case to be sure—lotus dreamers were not long for this world. It was a greater concern to the Cimmerian that Callidios and Mordermi were wont to remain closeted for long periods of time. Conan hoped Mordermi was using his wits to learn the secret of the Stygian's control of the Final Guard.

Out of one such tête-á-tête came the decision to despoil the tomb of King Kalenius. It was this even more than the summoning of the Final Guard to rout Korst's forces that impressed upon Conan Callidios' total mastery of the inhuman warriors. Callidios commanded the Final Guard to loot the tomb they had so long stood guard over.

Once the enormity of the plan was overlooked, the logic seemed obvious. Who better suited to loot a treasure vault than those who guarded it? Better still, these tomb-looters were impervious to the depths that covered the ancient barrow, nor could collapsed passages and unknown dangers within the king's eternal palace pose a threat to the Final Guard. It was an act of betrayal that outraged all honor—a betrayal of the dead king and a worse betrayal of the guardians who had endured living death for untold centuries to keep this tomb inviolate.

As Mordermi pointed out, the gold wasn't doing Kalenius any good. Conan was too much of a pragmatist to disagree, but the barbarian's lust for rich plunder notwithstanding, this was a treasure Conan wasn't sure might better remain hidden.

It was a macabre spectacle. Into the sea marched the Final Guard, and out of the depths they returned—bearing sealed chests and coffers of solid gold. In the millennia that had passed since King Kalenius had built his eternal palace, a great portion of his tomb's costly furnishings and treasure stores had decayed into dust and that dust dissolved into the sea. But if the exotic furs and exquisite carpets, the tapestries and paintings and carvings of rare woods, the opulent furniture and tables laden with choice viands were no more than smears of slime impinged upon the tiles of lapis lazuli — precious gems and costly metals had endured. Across the gulf of time that had decayed iron and bronze and rotted silver into blackened cinder, yellow gold and the eternally frozen starlight of diamonds, emeralds, rubies and a score of other rare gemstones were dragged from drowned darkness of the forgotten barrow and borne into the sunlight of a new age.

The procession was a drugged nightmare. Obsidian demons climbing out of the sea, bearing golden caskets whose contents represented the price of an empire. Only an army as dreadful as the Final Guard could have protected such a treasure from the avarice and greed of ages of seekers. The wealth they now laid before Mordermi would make his the richest court in all the Hyborian kingdoms.

Callidios had given Mordermi power; now he gave him wealth. Conan wondered what bargain the two of them had struck, and whether Callidios might have a third gift to bestow.

He took comfort from the fact that Callidios would no longer have a hold on Mordermi, once the Zingaran Revolutionary Army was strong enough to take the field. The Final Guard would not be needed then. Callidios, if he hadn't already wandered into his lotus dreams and lost his way back, could be dealt with in a final manner — and Mordermi's reign would be free of the taint of sorcery. To hasten this day, Conan redoubled his efforts with the new army.

Their situation remained a stalemate beyond the walls of

Kordava. The Final Guard preserved the city from any attack, but throughout the whole of Zingara Mordermi's rule was by no means secure. The powerful lords with their fortresses and personal armies might recognize Mordermi's claim to the throne or not, as they pleased. While the Final Guard was a force no human army could face in battle, Mordermi could not very well send his demon warriors marching off across Zingara to deal with those who defied his reign. While he might destroy their holdings, his enemies were certain to flee the advance of the stone warriors—and if he reduced the strength of the Final Guard by scattering them all across the countryside, Kordava would be open to a sudden attack.

Thus Mordermi needed his new army, and needed it quickly—before the outlying provinces decided there was no need to obey the commands of a usurper in distant Kordava. The threat of the Final Guard won for Mordermi some support beyond Kordava; the rich bribes he could offer purchased still more. But in the end, it would take an army in the field to consolidate his reign.

The threat to his rule was not long in materializing. Emboldened by Mordermi's refusal to commit the Final Guard beyond Kordava, Count Dicendo, who ruled extensive holdings on Zingara's distant eastern border, declared his lands to be an independent state. To support his claim, troops from neighboring Argos crossed the Khorotas River, in return for territorial concessions which Count Dicendo, having no authority to concede, made most generously from the lands of his rival, Baron Lucabos.

"We'll have to strike quickly and decisively, of course," Mordermi informed Conan of the situation. "Otherwise every landowner in Zingara will be declaring independence for his fishpond and barleyfields."

"The army is ready to fight," Conan told him with more confidence than he felt. "We'll be on our march at dawn."

"Good," Mordermi nodded. "I wish you a swift victory. Deal without mercy with these rebels. If we make an example of them, there are others who won't be so tempted to defy my authority. There's rumor that a conspiracy is brewing to the north, centering on some fool who claims to be Rimanendo's bastard. *That* would defy nature's law. Mitra, there's treason taking root in every corner of my kingdom!"

"You can depend on me," Conan said.

"I know that, Conan!" Mordermi seized his hand. "Mitra! If I had a hundred men like you to serve me!"

The Zingaran Revolutionary Army marched from Kordava the following dawn. The new army's general, on his first campaign, turned in his saddle, saw the black silhouettes of the Final Guard outlined against the graying skies. His scowl was troubled, but his concern was not for his new command.

XV. The Scythe

The season had changed from summer to autumn before
Conan returned to Kordava. It had been pleasant to see the
turn of the year from summer's dry heat to the autumn's
cool explosion of color. His stay in the Pit had been a season
of changeless twilight. Conan decided he had seen enough
of Kordava. Now that he had secured Mordermi's power
throughout Zingara, he would bid his friends here a farewell,
convert Mordermi's gratitude into a good horse and bag of
gold, ride northward toward Cimmeria. This being a general
of the king's army was not the sort of life that he wished
to follow to the end of his days. He was sick of fighting
another man's battles.

In the mountains of Zingara's eastern marches, Conan's
new army had waged a stubborn campaign over difficult
terrain, before Count Dicendo's stronghold was taken and
the rebellious count hanged outside the breached walls. By
that time Baron Lucabos, whose lands Dicendo had granted
to Argos in return for military support, was under siege and
strident in his requests for aid from his new liege lord.
Conan drove the Argosseans back across the Khorotas River,
proceeded after them, then was ordered back. Zingara's
invasion of Argos would be an act of war, Mordermi's
emissaries explained to him; the presence of Argossean sol-

diers on Zingaran soil did not have official sanction, and doubtless those responsible for the incident would be disciplined by their own king.

More to the point, a serious plot had gathered force in the north, as Mordermi had feared. A Poitanian adventurer named Capellas claimed to be the bastard son of Rimanendo and an Aquilonian noblewoman with whom the Zingaran king had dallied during a stay in Poitain. Capellas produced several passably forged documents to prove his claim, and since it was undeniably true that King Rimanendo had at one time passed through Poitain, royalists rejoiced to discover that a true heir to the throne of Zingara had been found. With a strong following of those of Rimanendo's court who had fled to exile in Aquilonia, Capellas crossed the Alimane River into Zingara—joined there by certain of the northern lords who had no especial loyalty to a usurper in Kordava when a pretender here at hand promised generous rewards for their support.

Capellas managed to lead his forces across half of Zingara, before Conan at length overtook him on the banks of the Thunder River. This was the sternest test yet for the Zingaran Revolutionary Army, as Capellas' were seasoned troops and the pretender was an experienced field commander. The battle raged in the balance throughout the long day, until Conan's mercenary reserves broke Capellas' flank and forced his routed troops into the river. Cutting off a limb to escape the trap, Capellas sacrificed his encircled troops and reteated northward with his cavalry. Conan gave pursuit once the invaders trapped against Thunder River had been annihilated, finally catching up with Capellas as he forded the Alimane to safety in Poitain. Conan had crossed at another ford, and met Capellas' cavalry in midstream. The depredations Conan had witnessed along the pretender's advance and retreat sealed the man's fate when Capellas protested that Conan's ambush had broken international treaty, and Capellas never crossed the Alimane.

Then came word that the savage Picts, whose tribes dwelt in the wilderness beyond Zingara's northwestern borders, had discovered that the frontier forts were no longer garrisoned, and were making bold raids along the Black River. Conan marched his weary troops across the northern frontier, knowing from experience that once the Picts decided they could cross the frontier with impunity, they'd burn every settlement between the border and Kordava. By forced marches the Zingaran Revolutionary Army reached the frontier in time to regarrison the forts that had been left to shift for themselves following the reorganization of the army. Several Pictish raiding parties, emboldened by past success, were intercepted and wiped out. The Picts retreated into their impenetrable wilderness, to wait for Zingara to doze again.

Thus when Conan at last returned to Kordava, he had been out of touch with events in the capital for many weeks. At times Mordermi had dispatched emissaries, other times vague gossip and rumors reached him. Conan had been on the move almost constantly, fighting all along the frontier. The Cimmerian had too much to worry about with his army to give a thought to the longwinded and pointless debates that were doubtless preoccupying the members of the revolutionary committee. Mordermi sent word to him where he was needed, and Conan had no curiosity beyond completing his task. Now, the hinterlands quiet if not peaceful, the Cimmerian elected to return to Kordava to reprovision and let his men enjoy a well deserved rest.

There had been changes during Conan's absence.

This became evident the moment Conan entered Kordava. A long row of wooden stakes had been set into the earth before the city's main gate. Impaled upon the stakes, decomposing human heads grinned crookedly at those who passed by. It was a common enough practice to display the heads of executed criminals in such a grisly fashion. Conan wondered whether Mordermi had decided to discontinue the old custom of leaving bodies swaying upon the Dancing Floor or whether the gallows had been too busy of late for this refinement.

The Cimmerian halted, doubting his eyes. Perhaps this was some distortion of decay. He knew it wasn't. One of the heads that greeted his return was that of Carico.

Conan continued to stare in disbelief. Ranging along the row of severed heads, he was able to recognize others whose faces he thought he knew—men he remembered as friends and followers of Carico.

Conan spurred his horse for the palace, after ordering his troops to their barracks. As he rode through the streets, he saw recent signs of civil strife. Shops stood broken-fronted and empty; crumpled walls showed the charred ends of timbers. An atmosphere of tension and fear overshadowed Kordava, where an aura of hope had existed at the time of Conan's departure. Squads of the Final Guard were stationed throughout the city, standing silently in readiness to destroy.

Conan had heard nothing of this—clearly a major riot had taken place very recently. Had there been no time to summon the army back to Kordava? Or had Mordermi been confident that the Final Guard could deal with the situation? And why the violence? Why was Carico's head given a felon's disgrace?

Mordermi would know the answers. Conan would find Mordermi.

The palace was closely guarded by the warriors of black stone as well as by a strong garrison of the Zingaran Revolutionary Army. Several officers whom Conan did not recognize rushed forward to receive their general and to escort him to Mordermi. As he moved through the palace, Conan could not fail to notice that during his absence Mordermi seemed to have renovated the looted palace on a scale of luxury Rimanendo would have envied.

Mordermi greeted Conan warmly and ushered him in to his private chambers. "You got back before I could reach you," he explained, pouring wine for the Cimmerian. "Things came to a head here the other night. Nothing I wasn't prepared to handle, but if I hadn't had the Final Guard to rely on, it might have been a different story."

Conan glared at Callidios, who lounged insouciantly in one of the chairs. "What happened?" Conan demanded. "I saw a sight I'd never thought to see outside the city gate."

"Then you can probably guess what took place," Mordermi told him, his tone expressing anguish. "They never could agree on anything—the revolutionary committee, that is. When the White Rose was no more than a debating society, it mattered little who argued what. When the White Rose suddenly was thrust in a position of power, and their philosophies could be put into effect—then their differing ideas as to their new order touched off deadlier dissension. It was building up at about the time you took the field.

"Avvinti maintained that only the landed classes should have a voice in government; Carico insisted that every man, beggar or lord, should have an equal vote. You've heard them go at it. I'd hoped that Santiddio might get them to accept some sort of compromise, but this was not to be."

Mordermi paused to take a swallow of wine. His face was bitter. "Avvinti was assassinated—poisoned. It was obvious that Carico had ordained his death. Just how deeply Carico had conspired became evident when I ordered his arrest. Carico's faction broke away from the revolutionary committee, began rioting in the streets demanding his release. I regret that Carico had decided that a second revolution would place him in power. It pained me to order his execution, but I was left with no choice. Callidios summoned the Final Guard to suppress the street riots. A certain amount of bloodshed was unavoidable, but order has been restored."

"And Santiddio?" Conan inquired grimly.

"Santiddio reacted in a rather hysterical manner when I was forced to dissolve the revolutionary committee and to declare martial law. This is purely an emergency measure to maintain order, of course, and one which I'm sure will be short term. However, Santiddio was not inclined to see reason. He began making some totally false accusations—very painful to me, considering our long friendship."

"What happened to Santiddio?" Conan pressed him.

"Under the circumstances, I had no recourse but to order his arrest. However unfounded and irrational such charges clearly are, I can't have a popular figure publicly accusing me of betraying the revolution for my own purposes."

"Just how unfounded and irrational are such charges?" Conan demanded.

"It's good that I know you are my friend, Conan. Otherwise that might have been a very dangerous attitude. As you yourself know best, I have enemies everywhere—at the borders of Zingara and here in my own palace. I've fought hard to win my throne, and I'm not about to let others steal what I have won."

"Carico might have fought Avvinti in the heat of anger," Conan mused, "but Carico was no poisoner. Those were some of Avvinti's wellborn friends in command of the palace guard, weren't they? Removing Carico must have set you in good with the gentry; Carico's talk of turning their estate over to the people had them worried."

Mordermi refilled Conan's goblet. "You know as well as I do that most of Carico's ideas were lunacy. And you're jumping to the same absurd conclusions that Santiddio did. You have to remember that words and actions taken out of context may have a sinister aspect that is utterly without real basis. For example, your defense of the barricades at Eel Street made you a hero. And yet, it has been reported to me that you actually deserted your post at one point, and

154

that you made a brash statement to the effect that if Mordermi wasn't standing by, you'd take command of the revolutionary movement yourself. Desertion and treason—taken out of context, of course, but grounds to order your arrest."

"Is that a threat?" Conan growled, starting forward. "Is that how Santiddio was arrested? Where is he, and let me talk to him!"

"That's already being arranged," Mordermi said truthfully. "I was afraid that primitive code of honor might cause problems in getting you to listen to reason."

Mordermi's voice echoed strangely, and his face seemed to blur. Conan snarled an angry reply, but his tongue felt thick. The Cimmerian glared at the goblet Mordermi had given him. It was too heavy to hold. Conan heard it crash to the floor, as he launched his body toward Mordermi. He never heard the sound of his own fall.

Mordermi looked down at the unconscious Cimmerian, his expression regretful. "Maybe after he's had time to sit and think about it, he'll be more reasonable. After all, he's no more than a barbarian adventurer. What does it matter to him whose cause he fights for, so long as it's the winning side?"

"You know better than that," Callidios said. He stirred the Cimmerian's loose form with a boot toe, admiring the effect of his craft. "He was your pawn because he trusted you. A king must know when a pawn is no longer of use to him."

XVI. The Reaper

Eventually there came a time when the blackness of his mind merged into the blackness of a dungeon cell. Conan lifted himself with his arms, retched as the effort stunned him with nausea.

"Here, drink some of this." Santiddio held a basin of tepid water to his lips.

Conan drank clumsily, his tongue dry and metallic. He rinsed his mouth and spat onto the filthy straw, seeking to cleanse the acrid taste from his mouth.

"So," said Santiddio. "Even you."

Conan made his eyes focus upon his surroundings. They were in one of the cells beneath the palace fortress. Faint torchlight trickled in from the corridor beyond. He and Santiddio were thrown together in a dirty cell barely large enough for one man. A thick door of iron-bound oak planks made up one side of the narrow cubicle, stone walls the others. A peephole was set with stout iron bars. There was a long row of such cells, with a guardroom at the end of the corridor that gave access to the dungeon stairs. At the other end was a torture chamber, kept in good repair during Rimanendo's reign. Conan remembered this dungeon well from what the victorious rebels had found here the night they stormed the tyrant's castle.

"What happened after I left Kordava?" Conan asked him, struggling to sit up against the dank wall.

"Everything went sour. We thought that all our dreams were coming true for us; the dream became a nightmare."

"Mordermi told me Avvinti was poisoned. I saw Carico's head impaled outside the city gate—Mordermi admitted to that murder. He claimed Carico was plotting a second revolution.'

"I've heard that tale. The people of Kordava didn't like it any better than you did. There were riots in the streets to protest Mordermi's arrest of the revolutionary committee— and that was when the devil sent out the Final Guard to restore order. Mordermi called the massacre he ordered a conspiracy by Carico and his faction."

"I can't understand this from Mordermi," Conan swore.

"Maybe none of us ever really knew what was going on in his head. Sandokazi thinks Callidios has some sort of hold over him. Callidios would be capable of anything."

Santiddio scratched at the raw scabs that crusted his face. They hadn't gulled him into a cell with a gift of drugged wine.

"I should have seen this coming," he said bitterly. "We accepted Callidios with open arms. Our cause was just; use any means to achieve its goal. Maybe our revolution would have been crushed without Callidios, maybe we could have beaten Rimanendo on our own in time. It never occurred to us that the same weapon could be used to crush our own cause. After all, Mordermi has been a champion of the common folk for years, and Callidios was a fellow revolutionary.

"Of course, in retrospect we were all probably too busy squabbling among ourselves to pay attention to anything other than our personal theories as to how the new government should be organized. I suppose that in time we'd eventually have come together in compromise. Mordermi took matters into his own hands, instead.

"He's discredited the White Rose by making it appear that we were each of us conspiring against the others. The great lords will follow any ruler who doesn't pose a threat to the present social order. They'd have been pleased to see Avvinti on the throne; certainly they'd never have accepted Carico's radical social changes. Even with the army, it would have been a long struggle just to enforce any moderate social reforms beyond Kordava. With this coup Mordermi removed a dangerous rival in Avvinti, then won the allegiance of the aristocracy by blaming the murder on Carico, dissolving the revolutionary committee, and destroying the White Rose under the pretense of restoring civil order. You can be certain that it wasn't coincidence that Mordermi waited until you were far in the field—winning his battles—before he made his move against us."

Santiddio seemed almost to admire the enormity of the coup. He shrugged his shoulders in resignation. "So Mordermi now looks like everything a king should be to the great lords. They'll not interfere with his reign now. You secured peace along the frontier for him. Now he'll simply move his officers into the army you put together for him. And he still has Callidios and the Final Guard. I think it will not be very long before we see Zingaran soldiers marching into Argos and Aquilonia."

"They may well so march," Conan allowed gloomily, "but I doubt we'll be here to see them. Mordermi knows he can't let us live after this. I'm surprised to be sitting here talking with you. It would have been just as easy to spirit the poison that Avvinti drank into my wine."

"Thus far Mordermi has sought to maintain a façade of legality to his actions," Santiddio suggested. "Sandokazi's plea spared my life thus far, I'm certain. Perhaps Mordermi hopes he can dupe you into rendering him some further service. But in time, once the people have forgotten the heroes of the Pit, we'll be tried on some invented charges, found guilty of treason, and sent to feed ravens on the Dancing Floor.''

Conan laughed without humor. "You and I have followed a long and difficult road, just to find ourselves walking in a circle. Are we two once again to stand together upon the Dancing Floor?''

"Well, I don't think we'd better count on Mordermi for our rescue this time,'' Santiddio grinned sourly.

"I think we may have owed that one to Sandokazi,'' Conan said. "What will happen to her now?''

"She has thrown her lot in with Mordermi,'' Santiddio sighed. "Not that I could expect her to join us in a cell, when she will wear a queen's crown if she remains with Mordermi. She loves the treacherous bastard, and she'll not desert him even now.''

"Nor will she stand by and let her brother rot in a cell,'' a new voice spoke.

Conan was on his feet in an instant, despite the stupor of the drug that still left his muscles rubbery.

Sandokazi peered in at them through the barred peephole. Her eyes held a wild, dreamy gaze.

" 'Kazi!'' Santiddio blurted. "Does Mordermi know you're here?''

"No, nor does anyone else,'' his sister smiled slowly. "He and Callidios are deep in schemes again. I'm certain Callidios wants him to order Conan's execution immediately, but Mordermi hasn't sunk so deep into the renegade's influence to agree that easily to a friend's murder.''

"Your lover's scruples in such matters are well known,'' Conan snarled. "He and I will share another drink to our friendship, but the wine will be of my choosing.''

"You mustn't blame Mordermi for what has happened,'' Sandokazi begged him. "Mitra, why didn't we heed your counsel when the Stygian first crept into our lives!''

160

"That's another mistake I'll see to when I get out of here," Conan vowed. "It was Mordermi who poured drugged wine for me."

"If it had been Callidios, you'd never have awakened," she argued fiercely. "How can you both be such fools! Mordermi was as deadly a foe of Rimanendo and his tyranny as any of us were. While we discussed ways of elevating the masses through social reform, Mordermi was distributing the spoils of his thefts to the poor. Callidios changed all this! I scarcely know Mordermi these days. That sorcerer has a spell over Mordermi. Kill Callidios, and Mordermi will be freed of his dark influence."

"What *are* you doing here, 'Kazi?" her brother asked again. "Did Mordermi send you to make a truce?"

"I'm here to set you free," Sandokazi explained, adding a wild giggle that made both men stare at her.

She held up a set of keys. "I've spied on Callidios," she told them, slurring her words somewhat. "I know where he keeps his precious yellow lotus. I dropped crumbs of the dried gum into the pipe bowl, as I've watch the Stygian do. But I crouched outside the guardroom door while they slumbered over their cups, and I blew the heavy fumes into the chamber. The air is still down here; the fumes grew deeper, and so did the snore of the guards. No one awoke when I crept in and stole the keys to the cells."

"Crom, woman!" Conan exploded. "Then let us out of here before the guards recover! What jest is this!"

"I'll let you out," Sandokazi said coyly. "But you must promise me that you won't kill Mordermi. I know he's betrayed all of us, but Callidios has poisoned his soul. Kill the Stygian, if you'll have your vengeance—but you both must give me your word that you won't kill Mordermi!"

Conan wondered how seriously the fumes of the yellow lotus had dazed the girl's wits. But there was no time to argue with her. The guards might be relieved, or the lotus-clouded girl might decide to withhold the keys out of spite.

"I promise not to kill Mordermi," Conan swore, although the oath burned in his throat. The Cimmerian would not break his word, no matter under what circumstances it was given.

"And I promise, as well," Santiddio conceded. "Now then, 'Kazi—be quick!"

For a maddening interval she fumbled for the proper key, struggled to work the massive lock. At length the bolts slid back. Conan went through the door like a great cat escaping its cage. He glared along the corridor, as Santiddio embraced his sister.

Within the guardroom, their wardens snored foolishly. Their lapse would doubtless cost them their lives, but Conan felt no remorse. The three chose military cloaks from a rack, and stole up the stairs.

There was a door at the top of the stairway, and beside the door a dead man. A thin-bladed dagger had expertly found his heart.

"I told him I'd make it worth his time to let me pass to visit my brother," Sandokazi explained. "He probably meant to renege afterward."

In the dead of night, the palace hallways were deserted except for patrolling guards. Conan had set the patrols, and with luck and stealth they were able to slip past them. Dawn, Conan knew, could not be far off; their escape would be discovered as soon as the guards were relieved.

"I have a rope hidden where you can descend the wall," Sandokazi told them. Conan had always admired her cleverness. "After you're beyond the fortress, you're on your own."

"You'll have to come with us," Santiddio urged. "Mordermi is certain to suspect you."

"Mordermi may suspect, but he'll do nothing," Sandokazi said. "Callidios may have poisoned his soul, but I still own his heart. Mordermi will blame your escape on the White Rose, and use it as further evidence of a conspiracy."

"You'll not hold us up, woman," Conan tried to argue. "I won't leave you here in danger after you've helped us. Mordermi isn't to be trusted . . ."

"Mordermi is my lover," Sandokazi snapped at him. "Can't you understand—I love him! If I run out on him now, he'll have no one beside him but Callidios."

Conan disagreed, but it was her decision to make. Santiddio knew better than to try to sway his sister's mind.

"What will you do?" she asked, drawing them away from the argument.

"Escape from Kordava to begin with," her brother answered. "We're too well known to hide out within the city, and Mordermi has too tight a grip here for us to challenge him. We'll organize a new rebellion from the ranks of the people he has betrayed—and this one won't be any trumped-up conspiracy for him to suppress as easily as he invented it."

"How will you stand again the Final Guard?" Sandokazi reminded them of the obvious.

"Do you have any knowledge of how Callidios controls his devils?" Conan asked her.

"Only that Callidios locks himself in a heavily guarded chamber atop the palace tower when he summons them," she told them. "And he doesn't reappear until their bloody task is completed. Callidios works all of his magicks there; no one is ever allowed to enter."

"We'll seek aid against the Stygian's sorcery from one who is also adept in the occult arts," Santiddio stated. "I've given the matter much thought, while staring at the walls of my cell."

"You'll seek aid from another sorcerer?" Conan protested. "If he has powers greater than those of Callidios,

163

we'll be turning the tiger into the house to drive out the wolf.''

"Not if she is our sister," Santiddio countered. "I'm going to ask Destandasi for her help—if she'll give it.''

Conan had all but forgotten that the Esantis were triplets, that their sister, Destandasi, had withdrawn from corrupt Zingara and entered the mysteries of Jhebbal Sag. Mordermi had told Conan that the third Esanti was a priestess in a sacred grove of Jhebbal Sag, somewhere beyond the Black River.

"Destandasi has cut all ties with our family—with the old traditions of Esanti greatness, and with the cause we two fight for today," Sandokazi said. "What reason for her to aid us now, even if she could.''

"I'm going to try," Santiddio frowned. "Where else can I turn to?''

"I'd a thought to cross the Black River to make our escape," Conan put in. "The border is close, and with the recent trouble with the Picts there, any guard along the northern marches will be a lot more concerned with who might be crossing from the Pictish Wilderness to care about who crosses over from Zingara. Can you find Destandasi?''

"I think I know how to find her," Santiddio said. "If not, we may as well let the Picts take our scalps as give Mordermi our heads.''

"We've wasted enough time then." Conan studied the skies. "If we hurry, we can steal a canoe and make our way well up the Black River before daylight.''

He tested the rope Sandokazi had provided, dropped it over the wall. "For the last time, will you come with us?''

"You know my decision. Just remember your promise to me.''

Conan considered clipping her on the chin and carrying her with them. But the woman had made her decision, and the Cimmerian respected her for it.

"Give Destandasi my love," she called out almost merrily, as they slid quickly down the rope and into the dark shadows at the base of the wall.

Sandokazi untied the rope and tossed it after them. No need to tell the guards which way the fugitives had fled. It was growing late, although the lotus fumes Sandokazi had inadvertently inhaled distorted her sense of time. Nonetheless, their stealthy passage to the outer wall and their whispered conversation had taken more time than seemed possible.

She made her way toward Mordermi's chambers, hoping that her lover was still in counsel with Callidios. If not— well, if he could stay awake to all hours, so might she. Sandokazi had an excuse in mind, when she remembered that she still carried Callidios' lotus pipe in her bodice.

She considered hiding it, but Callidios would mark its disappearance, connect it with the unconscious guards, and wonder why the conspirators who released the two prisoners had been so devious in their method. Best to return the pipe to its hiding place in Callidios' chambers, so that no one would ever guess how the guards had been drugged.

Sandokazi took care to make certain Callidios had not returned to his quarters. So much the better; he and Mordermi were still hatching schemes. Cautiously she slipped into the room and placed the pipe in its drawer next to the phial of yellow lotus.

She had forgotten that Callidios was also an illusionist.

Callidios stepped out of the grayness where the door had been a moment before.

"I can't sleep without it, of course," he said gently.

XVII. Destandasi

They had not paddled very far up the course of the Black River before Santiddio realized that he could never have attempted this journey and lived without the giant Cimmerian. For all that Conan was a close friend, while in Kordava Santiddio had never been able to put aside his air of easy superiority to the northern barbarian. It was part of the Kordavan manner toward those not fortunate enough to have lived in that city all their lives, and the Cimmerian, with his uncouth accent, his coarse manners and rustic ideas, had been too easy to regard as some uncultured boor from the provinces.

As they entered the outermost fringes of the Pictish Wilderness, Santiddio suddenly understood that here, as far removed from civilization as though Kordava were across the Western Sea and not merely a few days journey downstream, it was Conan who was the man of learning and he the untutored oaf.

They had stolen a canoe from along Kordava's riverfront. Seeming to have a cat's night vision, Conan had paddled fiercely upstream, not pausing until the climbing sun had burned the mist from off the river. Santiddio's lean frame was all sinew and wiry muscle, and he considered himself athletic enough. Yet long before Conan called a halt, his body ached as if it had been stretched upon the rack in Mordermi's dungeon. The Cimmerian had drawn the canoe alongside the shore, driven it beneath the thick willows that overhung the bank — carefully arranging a cover of branches.

"Too dangerous to go farther by day," he explained, as if to a child. "Mordermi will remember that once I thought to flee Rimanendo's hangmen by crossing into the Pictish Wilderness. He can send mounted patrols along the river-bank and cover ground faster than we can paddle upstream. By night we can slip past them, so long as we keep to the moonshadows."

Santiddio had sprawled out upon the floor of the canoe, sleeping soundly despite the cramped position. When he awoke, Conan gave him a handful of nuts and some autumnal fruit he had gathered along the riverbank; Santiddio had never sensed it when the Cimmerian had left the canoe.

With dusk they continued upstream. Conan paddled in a more regular rhythm now, but each time Santiddio stabbed the water with his paddle, fire seemed to lance through every muscle. Once Conan halted the canoe, signed for silence; they remained in the shelter of a half-submerged snag for what must have been an hour, until Conan cautiously resumed paddling.

"The other canoe," Conan explained to him later. "Didn't you see them drift past us? Mordermi should tell his hounds not to wear mail if they can't sit without motion."

Santiddio had seen, had heard nothing.

The next day Conan was able to spear a carp with a dagger he had attached to a pole. They had taken swords and daggers from their guards, but there had been no bow or quiver of arrows with which they might take game. Raven-ously devouring his portion of the raw fish, Santiddio realized that the Cimmerian could fashion some sort of rough bow and arrow if the need arose.

Another night's paddling took them past burned-out clearings where the stench of smoke still hung on the night air. "We won't have to worry about Mordermi's patrols any farther upstream," Conan laughed harshly. "The Picts have raided this far south, and these Zingarans won't risk running into any raiding parties that might have been slow to return without a fresh belt of scalps."

Conan dug his paddle into the river with renewed energy. "From here on in," he said, "we're going to have to be ten times more careful."

The next evening, just before they started northward again, Conan emerged from the forest with a short bow of dark wood and a quiver of flint-tipped arrows. He placed these carefully at hand in the canoe, then passed Santiddio a leather pouch of dried meat and some coarse cake made of acorn meal.

"I took pains to sink it, but Picts are devils when it comes to finding their dead. Let's hope he didn't have any friends close by," Conan told him in a near whisper. "We need to make some distance now."

There was a trading post situated along the Black River at the vague point where Zingara's frontier was presumed to end and the edges of the Pictish Wilderness to begin. Since the Picts had never been known to recognize the boundaries that learned men drew on maps, the border was a tenuous point. The trading post was run by a half-breed named Inizio, and whether because of his Pictish blood or his usefulness as a trader, the Picts generally left him alone. Letters, when they had come, from Destandasi had reached them by stages that led back to here, and letters they had sent to their elusive sister had been directed toward Inizio's post, whence presumably they eventually reached Destandasi.

Conan thought that Inizio's trading post had not been burned during this most recent series of raids. They would take up the trail from there.

Inizio had taken on the peculiar dwarfish physique that seemed to result when Pictish blood mixed with the Hyborian races. Unlike most proprietors of such frontier waystations, his manner was taciturn, his attitude almost hostile. Santiddio wondered if the trader preferred to have dealings with the Picts, or whether he resented all intrusions upon his solitude here.

When Santiddio explained his mission, Inizio had only glared at them. Conan glowered back, and after a moment beneath that, Inizio shrugged his thick shoulders and admitted: "The letters came out of the forest, I sent them downstream; the letters came upriver, I sent them into the forest."

"And who carried them in and out of the forest?" Santiddio asked patiently.

Inizio's scowl darkened. "An owl."

"An owl?"

"That's right. A big damn owl."

"You mean like a carrier pigeon?" Santiddio pressed him.

"Like that. Flies at night, beats the door with its wings. Letter tied to its leg."

"And comes to carry letters back to its mistress. How does it know when to come?"

"I don't want trouble. I don't want trouble with nothing."

"Then answer when you're asked something," Conan advised.

"Cimmerian Pict-Slayer," Inizio grunted, "I don't scare of you. I don't scare of soldiers. I don't scare of Picts. I don't want no trouble."

"Write a letter to your sister, Santiddio," Conan suggested. "Tell her you're here and why. Ask her to meet us here or send a guide. Inizio will make certain it gets to her, since we'll wait here with him until we get her reply."

At midnight there came the beat of wings upon the door of the trading post. Inizio unbarred the door, and a huge owl flew into the room. Conan, who could name almost

170

any bird or animal that was to be found here, had never seen an owl such as this one. The black-feathered bird regarded them with a scowl not unlike Inizio's, while the trader tied the message to its leg. Then, with an almost silent thrust of its great wings, the owl was out of the doorway and vanished into the night.

They never were able to learn how Inizio had summoned the owl.

Conan was thoughtfully honing the edge of his sword the following evening, when a wolf appeared in the dusk and loped purposefully toward Santiddio. Conan's first thought was that the animal was a pet of Inizio, so calm was its self-assurance. The wolf turned its yellow eyes upon the Cimmerian, and Conan knew this beast had never been tamed. Behind them, he heard the trader slam and bar his door.

There was a thong tied about the wolf's massive neck, and a letter was fastened to the thong.

Santiddio read it once to himself, then aloud for Conan's sake: "My brother: I have taken a vow never to leave this sacred grove. If you must see me, this messenger will lead you to me. I must warn you that you will be trespassing upon a region where the old gods are more than memory. I advise you to return to the world where you belong. Destandasi."

"What do we do?" Santiddio wondered, still puzzling over the message. "Do we follow my sister's pet?"

"We follow," Conan agreed. "And that wolf is no pet."

They left the clearing, and in a moment the trading post and all evidences of man's work had vanished behind a darkening wall of tall trees.

Another mile, and the darkness had so deepened that neither man could see the trail they followed—if indeed a trail existed beneath the black columns of the trees. Santiddio rested his hand lightly on the wolf's hackles, trusting the beast to lead them to whatever awaited them. Conan gripped his swordhilt and listened uneasily to the sounds that followed them through the darkened forest. He knew that they need not fear Picts on this night journey, but that knowledge held no reassurance for him.

They were alone in the midst of a forest that had been ancient when Conan's ancestors had squatted in caves and brooded upon the mystery of fire. The Pictish Wilderness was a trackless ocean of forest and mountains; no man of the white races had ever traversed it, even the savage Picts had never penetrated vast sections of the forestland. Time and distance became meaningless concepts—human and therefore meaningless—as they walked on and on between boles whose girth ten men could not encompass, upon a carpet of forest mould that swallowed the sound of their footsteps. But for the presence of their feral guide, they might have been two damned souls adrift in limbo.

"A region where the old gods are more than memory," Destandasi had warned them. Truly as they walked through this primeval forest, Conan realized that these trees shared the antiquity of the very rocks beneath their roots. It was an awful sensation when a living presence exuded the frightful antiquity of the earth itself.

There was suddenly a distant glimmer of light through the forest ahead of them, and Conan had never greeted a dawn with deeper joy.

It was a small clearing, although after the claustrophobic passage between the gigantic columns of trees, the clearing seemed a living island of space and of light. A woman stood within the clearing, awaiting their coming. It was a moment before Conan looked beyond her.

Conan had pondered in the course of their journey as to what the remaining sibling of the Esanti triplets would look like. Aloof, Mordermi had described her, and sharing the features of sister and brother. Conan had envisioned a sort

172

of skinny Sandokazi with the cold sneer of a maiden queen. He had not expected the Destandasi who greeted them here in this lost grove.

Strangely enough, she did make him think of both Sandokazi and Santiddio. Destandasi was tall and straight, neither thin nor buxom. Her face called to mind Sandokazi, with its dark complexion and glowing eyes whose dark pupils seemed larger than the normal. Again the angular chin and high-bridged nose, but her lips smiled bitterly where Sandokazi's were roguish. Her shoulders were straight and almost mannish, her breasts small and high, her hips slender—as opposed to her sister's generous display of curves. She might have been a sister of some years younger to compare their figures, but her face made her seem an equal span of years older then Sandokazi. Her hair was of lustrous black highlights, and she wore it gathered into one long fall that trailed down over one breast to her waist. Her gown was of some dark green material—a simple affair that was tied at her shoulders and fell straight to her bare calves, gathered at the waist by scarlet cord. She was barefoot despite the chill of an autumn night.

Conan thought of her as a dryad or a virginal wood sprite, and when he looked elsewhere in the clearing, he decided his first impression was a true one. There was a colossal elm—ancient beyond calculation—squatting upon one edge of the clearing. The bole could not have been encircled by ten tall men with arms outstretched and joined, and, as sometimes occurred with trees of this age, its trunk was hollow. A gap between two huge root buttresses made a doorway; crevices where the heartwood had rotted out of the scars of lost branches made windows. Like a dryad, Destandasi lived within a tree. There was a small spring near the center of the clearing. A small fire burned upon slabs of stone not far from the base of the hollow elm, and lamplight peered through the crevices and doorway.

Conan thought brother and sister embraced one another with more restraint than the circumstances allowed for. "Welcome to my home, brother," Destandasi greeted him with equal formality.

"Destandasi, this is Conan. He's been a tremendous friend to both Sandokazi and me—as you'll soon learn."

"Welcome, Conan," she said, giving him her hand. "I hope you will neither of you regret your coming here."

Under the circumstances, Conan wasn't certain whether to kiss her hand or clasp it. He chose the latter, was glad he did, for she returned his grasp with a strength that belied the aloofness of her smile.

"Will you enter my home? I have set out food and drink."

As formal as a hostess. Or a priestess.

And who but a priestess could endure the awful loneliness of this grove—no, not endure, rather cherish it.

Conan wondered where the worshippers might be on this night.

XVIII.   A Sending From Kordava

Santiddio talked while they ate. Talked to such length and feeling that Conan wondered how he remembered to take a mouthful of food.

The food was simple fare of breads and cakes of coarse-ground grains and nuts, baked upon her stone oven outside the tree, accompanied by a soup of different vegetables, along with fruits and roasted nuts. Conan recognized most of the ingredients as coming from various wild plants. It was all well prepared and quite filling, although Conan guessed that the absence of meat was deliberate. Recalling what little he knew of the mysteries of Jhebbal Sag, this came as no surprise.

The interior of the hollow elm was extremely cozy, and with its vertical dimensions, afforded far more interior space than Conan had expected. Destandasi's possessions were few and simple, most of them evidently of her own making. A small loom took up some space, as did a table and cabinets of utensils and materials she used to make the things she needed. A few books made almost a discordant note. Shelves and niches were everywhere around the interior of the hollow bole. Steps cut into the trunk gave access to a bed laid out on a narrow shelf framed into the interior of the bole overhead from where they sat. Lamps of pine oil made a mellow light, and there was a stone slab by one knothole where small fires might be laid. Heavy curtains could shut off the doorway and windows.

Conan did not like to think about a woman living alone in the Pictish Wilderness with no more than a curtain to shut out an intruder. As he thought more about it, the Cimmerian decided that the priestess of Jhebbal Sag would not be in danger from any attacker—man or beast—here in the sacred grove. Conan was an experienced woodsman, yet the Cimmerian sensed that had the wolf not guided them to this grove he and Santiddio might have wandered forever beneath the inimical shadow of the forest.

Santiddio brought his narrative to a close with the account of their reaching Inizio's trading post. Destandasi had listened almost without interruption throughout the tale, only her glowing eyes evincing any interest.

"What do you expect of me?" she asked bluntly, when it was evident that her brother was awaiting some response.

Santiddio waved his hand about the room in a vague gesture. He pointed toward her books.

"You've delved into the occult," he accused her. "Before you chose to lose yourself in the deepest wilderness the gods ever created, you studied other paths than the one you at last followed."

"This is not a place for flippancy," Destandasi said quickly—and it was a warning, not a scolding.

"But you did study such matters," Santiddio pursued. "You must have some inkling as to how we can defeat Callidios, how we can fight against the Final Guard."

"I turned my back on all such matters when I became a priestess of Jhebbal Sag," Destandasi reiterated.

"Well, you can't just turn your back on your brother and sister also," Santiddio protested. "We still live out there in the world of man and man's cities."

"I took a vow never to leave this grove."

"Then stay here in your tree," Santiddio said hotly. "I came to you because I need your advice."

"My advice is for both of you to leave Kordava. There's nothing there to hold you. Kordava holds only doom for the Esanti blood."

"Kordava is the home of the Esantis. I, too, have certain vows and ties that bind me to Kordava. I've got to return to complete the work Mordermi has betrayed. All I'm asking for is some means to counter Callidios' sorcery so that we can meet Mordermi on equal terms."

Destandasi pressed her lips together in thought. "From what you've told me, I have no idea how Callidios can command the Final Guard. The wizards who created them might have the power to usurp control over them, but this Callidios can't have powers of that degree. If he did, be certain that he'd never have needed to play along with Mordermi and the White Rose. I suspect that what he has told you is the truth—that he has no formal apprenticeship in the black arts such as any archimage must endure, but that on his own growing up in the temple of Set he succeeded in developing some specialized power or talent to a high degree. A sort of dabbler in all sorceries and an adept in one."

"That doesn't tell us anything," Santiddio said tiredly.

"I've told you all I can. This isn't my area of study by any means. The mysteries of Jhebbal Sag concern life forces. We are the few who *remember*—the last few."

" '*Remember*'?" Conan repeated her stress on the word.

"There is little I may tell you, less that you would understand," Destandasi said carefully. "There was an age when *all* living things worshipped Jhebbal Sag, and men and beasts were brothers who spoke one language. Only a few have retained that memory—beasts more so than men. It is a memory that can be reawakened. More than this I may not disclose."

"But you can't help us defeat the Final Guard with your knowledge?" Santiddio asked in dejection.

"I have studied living things, sought to understand the unity of all life. You want to learn about the forces of death and of chaos. Go to a sorcerer."

"That's the dilemma," Santiddio sighed. "Assuming we were able to enlist the aid of a magician whose powers were greater than Callidios'—then we'd run the risk of his seizing control of the Final Guard."

"Better the devil you know," Destandasi finished for him. "I'm sorry, but I honestly don't know how to advise you in this."

A scream from the clearing outside ripped apart the brooding silence that had set in after her words. It was at once a howl of baffled rage and a shrilling of agony. Conan was not certain whether the cry was human or bestial, and in this grove the distinction might not be all that clear cut.

Destandasi came to her feet in one fluid movement. Her face expressed shock and uncertainty. Conan gave her a single glance, understood that this was not the cry of one of the children of Jhebbal Sag, and was through the door with drawn sword in the next instant.

The Cimmerian skidded away from the pool of light, crouched low against the massive bole, as he searched the clearing for the source of the outcry. Something white struggled frantically at the opposite edge of the clearing. Conan made for it in catlike bounds, keeping low.

A woman stood at the edge of the sacred grove. It was Sandokazi.

Conan stood gaping for a moment, as Santiddio and Destandasi caught up to him. Sandokazi stared back at him wildly.

"Mitra! It's 'Kazi!" Her brother recognized her face in the wan light. "Did you change your mind and decide to join us after all? How did you manage to find us? Poor 'Kazi, no wonder you . . .''

He started forward to embrace her, but Destandasi hauled him back from her reach. "No! Keep back from her!" she hissed.

Sandokazi made a low growl, tried to edge forward. Some force was holding her back.

"Don't you see!" Destandasi's voice was sick. "She can't cross the circle of the sacred grove!"

Conan's eyes adjusted from the light within the tree home to the near darkness at the edge of the forest. His brain now registered that which his instincts had warned him of an instant before.

Sandokazi wore only a filthy shift. Her bare feet were torn and scratched, her tangled hair matted with briars and muck. Instead of a pearl necklace, a hempen noose bit into her throat—left there in a cruel jest. Her neck seemed unnaturally long, tipped crookedly away from the knot. Her eyes protruded in a ghastly stare, emanating insensate malice. Her tattered lips writhed in an animal snarl, and as she clawed at them from the edge of the circle, they could smell the sweet taint of decay.

"Can't you see?" Destandasi's voice was shaken but her nerve was steady. "She's dead. They killed her, and Callidios sent her on your trail to kill you. If you'd been camped along the river, she would have attacked you like a deadly beast. She would leap upon us now, if evil sendings could cross the sacred grove."

Santiddio knelt, retching between the sobs that tore from him as if hot nails had been driven into his breast.

Conan raised his sword to strike. His face was terrible with the rage he could not express.

"Don't!" Destandasi checked him. "That isn't the way. She's dead—a dead thing that Callidios controls! The Stygian has revealed to us where his genius lies: Callidios is a master of necromancy.''

''What can I do!'' Conan groaned between clenched teeth.

''Take Santiddio away from this and stay with him. There is a sign of power that I may use to break this foul spell. It would not be good if you saw what I do now, for the secrets of Jhebbal Sag are jealously guarded.''

''I'm not afraid,'' Conan swore. ''I'll stay to help you . . .''

''Leave me with that which was my sister!'' Destandasi hissed. ''Haven't you already helped her!''

Conan swallowed a retort. Picking up Santiddio as if he were some broken doll who might shatter completely, Conan left Destandasi to do what must be done.

XIX. Dreams Are Born to Die

They buried Sandokazi within the sacred grove at daybreak.

Conan dug the grave beneath the graying skies of dawn. He flung back the earth, his breath jerking in savage grunts with each blow of the shovel. From the blaze in his eyes, he might have been striking against living flesh.

Destandasi quietly washed the desecrated body of her sister—now exorcised of its depraved sham of life—and prepared a shroud from the coverlets of her bed. Her face was lined with a stress beyond even this horror, and Conan guessed that the powers of Jhebbal Sag were not to be invoked without a price.

Santiddio remained silent throughout the ordeal. Looking into his eyes, Conan knew that the soul of adventurous youth had gone into the grave with Sandokazi.

As the Cimmerian threw the final spadeful of earth upon the grave, Santiddio found his voice. "I don't care any longer whether our cause is a lost one, or whether the final victory will be ours. I only know that I return now to Kordava to continue the struggle, and that I'll send that Stygian down into the Hell that spawned him if it's the last thing I do!"

"I'm going to Kordava with you," Destandasi stated.

"But your vow!" her brother reminded.

"There comes a time when vows must be broken." Des-

181

tandasi bent to place a spray of dried flowers and autumn leaves upon the grave.

"All living things are sacred to Jhebbal Sag," she continued. "It is wrong to take a life. It is an unspeakable sacrilege to enslave a dead soul by animating its clay with a hideous mockery of life. It was a great evil that Callidios did to Sandokazi. Such evil must not be permitted to endure."

"Then you *can* help us defeat Callidios' sorcery?" Conan asked quickly.

"I believe I have fathomed the secret of his command of the Final Guard," Destandasi announced. "If I have, it may be that Sandokazi will be avenged—for in sending her forth as one of the walking dead to perform his commands, Callidios may have revealed himself. Had you any suspicion that the Stygian was a necromancer?"

"Callidios is secretive and devious in everything," Conan replied. "He belittles the demonstrations of his powers that he has revealed on occasion, boasts of his mastery of dark forces that remain his secret."

"His mastery of necromancy would justify his boasts. It demands the most potent spells in order to raise the dead and compel them to reveal the course of future events. Callidios, it seems, has exceeded the depraved ambitions of most others who delve into the necromantic arts. Callidios not only has the power to raise the dead, but he can compel the reanimated corpse to obey him in whatsoever he shall command. Sending Sandokazi across Zingara to slay those whom she loved was as arrogant a stroke as it was cruel. He meant that you should know in the moment of your death that the dread powers he boasted to possess were all that he had claimed."

Santiddio thought upon her words, trying to follow her line of reasoning. "Then you believe that Callidios can command the Final Guard through necromancy? But the

182

Final Guard are no reanimated liches; if Callidios spoke the truth, the stone devils are virtually deathless. The wizards of ancient Thuria created them to obey only King Kalenius; to guard his tomb throughout eternity was Kalenius' command to them.''

''I believe that the Final Guard continues to obey only King Kalenius,'' Destandasi concluded.

''But Kalenius is dead!''

''True. Even as Sandokazi is dead.''

They stood mute as the understanding of her logic came to them. Destandasi laid it out for them, as their minds reeled with the enormity of it.

''Callidios learned of the tomb of Kalenius through writings he perused in the temple of Set in Stygia. He told Conan that the body of Kalenius had been preserved by the king's sorcerers and set upon a golden throne to rule his eternal palace. Kalenius was obsessed with his tomb; if his sorcerers were capable of creating the Final Guard, one can assume the same effort was devoted to the preservation of the king's mortal remains.

''Callidios sought out the tomb of Kalenius, discovered that his knowledge was true. I doubt that even a necromancer of his powers could have reanimated a corpse that had disintegrated into dust and its dust dissolved into the sea. But Kalenius' sorcerers had done their work too well. Callidios must have summoned Kalenius to come forth from his tomb—using his power to raise the dead—and the ages-dead king became a slave to the Stygian necromancer.

''Thus: Kalenius commands the Final Guard. And Callidios commands Kalenius.''

''Can you be certain of this?'' Santiddio wondered.

''No. It is only supposition, based upon what you have told me and what we have endured. But I believe this to be correct—that herein lies the secret of Callidios' power. You came here to seek my counsel; you have heard it.''

"We came to discover how the Final Guard might be defeated," Conan put in. "Does this mean you have knowledge of a weapon that we might use? Tell us, and remain in your grove in peace."

"Not a weapon, but a weakness in their armor, Conan. And I must strike the blow myself, for only I have the power. We must find the corpse of King Kalenius, so that I may exorcise the evil sham of life with which Callidios has possessed it, as I did with my sister's violated flesh. Without Kalenius, Callidios cannot command the Final Guard."

"Without the Final Guard, Mordermi cannot hold Koradava against us," Santiddio stated with confidence. "Which means Callidios will have guarded his secret carefully."

"And without Callidios, Mordermi cannot rely on his army of devils," Conan pointed out. "Assassination or exorcism, either attempt will be guarded against."

"Sever either link, and the chain is broken. This doubles our chances. Moreover, Callidios may not suspect that we have penetrated his secret."

"I only pray that I have guessed correctly," Destandasi said. "Has there been anything to suggest that Callidios has possession of Kalenius' lich? Has no one seen such a thing?"

"Callidios works his spells from a tower chamber to which no one is admitted, so Sandokazi told us," Conan said. "When the Final Guard slaughtered Korst's soldiers in the Pit, Callidios was not to be seen. Earlier, he and Mordermi had talked together in secret. Mordermi came from that closet confident of victory; he knew that the Final Guard had been summoned when he led his forces to the battle in Eel Street. Callidios was not seen again until after Rimanendo's palace had fallen, and the Final Guard were no longer needed to cheat the crowd of its share in the massacre. I asked Mordermi to halt them, and he responded

184

that only Callidios knew the secret of their control.

"There are sewers and passages beneath the Pit through which the sea courses in high tide. I've smelled the sea close to me in Mordermi's stronghold, and he told me once that so long as his rats could swim, they need have no fear of being trapped there. Callidios frequented the waterfront, seeking clues of the tomb's location. He may have already discovered where the sea flowed beneath Mordermi's stronghold, or Mordermi may have shown him after the two made their pact. If what you think is true, Callidios could have descended into such a passage, cast his spells in secret there, and summoned Kalenius to leave his golden throne and come forth from his sunken barrow to join the sorcerer in the sewers beneath the Pit.

"Kalenius may still be hidden there, or Callidios may have bidden him return to his barrow. Or, since it is through Kalenius that the Stygian wields his power, Callidios may have spirited his slave into his tower chamber. When the Final Guard stripped Kalenius' tomb and bore its treasures into Mordermi's palace, they brought many strange coffers out of the depths. One of these may have enclosed the lich of their king."

"Almost certainly the corpse would be in Callidios' tower," Destandasi agreed. "There the Stygian can watch over it; command it to his will when the Final Guard must be summoned. Well reasoned, Conan. You may have described all that took place in fact. Everything you have said bears out my supposition."

"Then we must break into Callidios' tower and know for truth," Conan said, having far more faith in direct action than in relying upon theories.

"It is I who must enter the tower," Destandasi said quietly. "I shall need a moment to prepare for our journey."

Santiddio knelt beside the grave as they waited. Conan withdrew to give him the privacy of his farewell. Santiddio's

185

lips were working, but from his eyes Conan did not think the youth was praying.

The Cimmerian gazed about the sacred grove, seeking to escape the bitterness of his own thoughts. The grove was a haven of natural beauty and serenity; its aura of peacefulness could not soothe the pain he felt. Conan knew that only red battle and the dark flames of vengeance could give his soul release.

Destandasi was not long in her leavetaking. When she rejoined them, she had donned sandals and a travelling cloak, and carried a small pack of her possessions. She handed a basket to Santiddio.

"Food for our journey," she said simply. "I am ready to leave."

"Can you not bar your door?" Santiddio asked uneasily.

"Why should I? Who shall come when I have gone?"

She took a final look about the sacred grove, at the spring and her hearth, at the giant elm wherein she had made her home a part of nature. Her eyes glowed with emotion, and her lips tightened as she gazed at the last upon the grave.

"I sought to find a sanctuary from the evil in our world. I found it here in the grove of Jhebbal Sag. I vowed never to leave this haven. But evil has revealed its presence to me even here, and I must break my vow to erase the shadow it has flung across the grove."

"Afterward," Santiddio said awkwardly, "you can come back to your grove and dwell here in peace."

"Ah, no. I shall never return. Only once in the life of a soul is sanctuary revealed. Once renounced, it shall be forever lost."

XX. The Road of Kings

In the weeks that followed tales of increasing civil unrest coupled with unbridled tyranny reached them as they travelled. In return for their support of his reign, Mordermi gave the great lords a free hand to rule their holdings as they willed. In Kordava, the new king's taste for show and luxury made his palace and court the most magnificent of all the western realms, while his court revels were rumored to exceed even the debauches of the most licentious eastern potentates.

The bribes he bestowed lavishly, the costs of his growing mercenary army, the expense of his opulent court—all made inroads on a treasure even so seemingly limitless as the loot of Kalenius' tomb. Reluctant to deplete his trove unnecessarily, Mordermi simply doubled taxation beyond Rimanendo's excesses of the past. Protest was viciously suppressed, and disturbances were crushed without mercy. Backed by the presence of the Final Guard, Mordermi's rule was unassailable and absolute.

Zingara seethed with popular unrest as never before—for the threat of the Final Guard made Mordermi arrogant in his power, knowing that any act of oppression he chose to make must be endured by his subjects. To resist was to die.

There are times when existence may grow so intolerable

that even the threat of death loses its terror. Through this mounting desperation, Conan and Santiddio moved across Zingara, gathering men for their cause—secretly at first, then openly calling the people to arms as their ranks swelled. Conan had been well liked by his men—many of whom had been in open disbelief when it was announced that their general had been arrested for treason—and Mordermi's picked henchmen who took over from Conan's officers were resented. Conan now was able to win over whole garrisons from the men who had followed him before and who now mutinied against Mordermi's officers. The mercenary companies, who saw Conan as a hero from their ranks, came over to the Cimmerian in entire units. At the same time, Santiddio addressed the common people of every city and village, calling for them to rise up against those who oppressed them and to push the revolution Mordermi had betrayed on to final victory. Santiddio had always been a clever public speaker, albeit frequently too intellectual for the audience he addressed. Now his words were driven into their minds by the naked emotions that raged in his heart. Once Santiddio had sought to instruct the people; now he inflamed them.

Word of Conan's growing power in the provinces reached Mordermi in Kordava. The king sent out an expedition commanded by the powerful Count Perizi to intercept the rebels and destroy their army. Conan retreated into the eastern mountains. When Perizi confidently pursued, Conan struck from ambush with far greater strength than his feigned retreat had evidenced. Perizi was defeated after a day of hard fighting, and enough of his expeditionary force escaped to spread tales of a powerful rebel army whose strength was anything but the ragged guerilla band they had been told to destroy. After that, Conan's army doubled its ranks in days. No longer did the rebels move secretly; the great lords retreated into their fortresses and prayed their army would be content to pass by.

Concern deepened in Kordava. Mordermi sent out a major army under Baron Manovra. Conan sent him back Manovra's head. The rebels were now in control of the provinces.

Mordermi's followers pleaded with him to send the Final Guard into the field to annihilate the rebel army. Mordermi refused, pointing out that this would be playing into Conan's hands. The rebels could not control Zingara unless they took Kordava, and they could not take Kordava because of the Final Guard. Conan's strategy was to ravage the provinces, seeking to draw the Final Guard out of Kordava. Once the Final Guard had been lured into the provinces, the rebels could sweep down on Kordava and attack the city before the stone warriors could march back.

In time, Mordermi argued, Conan's rebels would grow impatient. Emboldened by their victories, they would at last move against Kordava and seek the final victory. Then Conan would have played into Mordermi's hands, and the massacre of the rebels that day would end thoughts of revolution for all time.

Mordermi again proved to be a master of strategy. Word came to Kordava that Conan was marching against the capital.

Santiddio's face was as hard as his steel cuirass, as he went over final preparations for the next day's battle. It was a battle that he must lead.

"You've seen more combat than most king's generals," Conan rallied him. "Trust Vendicarmi here if you're uncertain as to any move. This old warhorse has fought in more battles than I have, and I was born on a battlefield."

Conan grinned at the frost-bearded mercenary captain who shared their council, then grew more serious. "One of us has to lead tomorrow's attack. Otherwise the men will believe we've deserted them in the face of the Final Guard. It is bad enough that I won't be in the front of things, that I'll supposedly be leading a charge against the river gate. But we dare not trust the secret of our mission to others; surprise is our only chance for success.''

"I only wish I were going with you," Santiddio said. "Or instead of you. You could remain here and lead the attack.''

"The attack is a feint—I hope you've understood that much! *Don't* close with the Final Guard. Harass the walls, seek to draw them out. Mordermi will expect that, withhold his army of devils. Let the stalemate stand. When Mordermi finally wearies of this and sends the Final Guard into the field—fall back! You can't do battle with them, so stay clear. Let them chase you all the way to Aquilonia, but don't throw away brave men's lives against devils that can't be slain.

"My mission will be two-fold," Conan went on. "To kill Callidios and to get Destandasi into his tower. One or the other, I must not fail. I'm not saying a thing against you, Santiddio—but if it comes down to cutting through a ring of guards to get to Callidios, I'll take a lot of killing before I'm down.''

He clasped Santiddio's hand. "If we make it, *and* if we've guessed right, the Final Guard will be no more. Then you can throw every man you've got against the soldiers that remain, and good luck. If the Final Guard marches from Kordava, then you'll know I'm dead. You'll have to try again.''

"Good luck to you, Conan. I'll see you in Kordava, or I'll see you in Hell.''

Conan and Vendicarmi paused outside the tent, while Santiddio spoke a few words with Destandasi. Their parting was short. In a moment the girl stood beside Conan and nodded.

Together they slipped through the darkened camp. A group of horsemen awaited them at the perimeter—ostensibly the advance scout that Conan had ordered to examine the defenses of the river gate. They were trusted men, sworn to secrecy. When Conan and Destandasi left their party in the course of their ride, no head turned to follow them.

Kordava slept fitfully, awaiting the battle that the next day would bring. Confident that the Final Guard would defend the city for them, the sentries along the walls maintained their watch with a casualness born of arrogance. Victory would certainly be theirs—a victory won for them by the demon warriors—and only a fool would spill his own blood.

Others within Kordava felt only despair during this eve of battle. Their hopes were with the rebels, and tomorrow would see the annihilation of their army and of their cause. Mordermi's rule would never again be challenged after tomorrow.

Conan had slipped past far more vigilant sentries than those who kept watch along Kordava's waterfront. Beside him, Destandasi moved with the silent stealth of a forest creature. They had left their horses at a distance; Conan stole a skiff, and they drifted into the waterfront under the chill cover of mist. Where the fires had burned themselves out after the battle of the Pit, little had been done to rebuild the devastated slum area. Like ghosts the two edged through the chaos of blackened walls and charred timbers—at length descending by a devious entrance into the Pit.

The appearance of two cloaked figures in the Pit was nothing that would draw attention, even on this night when the usual air of revelry was stifled by the approaching battle. Conan's chief fear was that he would be recognized—he was well known here, and his giant frame stood out. Avoiding the rare patches of light, Conan hoped no hostile eyes would penetrate the shadows of his hood. Chances were that the citizens of the Pit sympathized with the rebels, but that wouldn't stop one of them from collecting the generous bounty Mordermi would pay to learn of Conan's whereabouts on the eve of his attack. The fact that everyone knew that Conan would lead his rebel army against Kordava within the next several hours dulled the suspicions of any who may have taken note of the hulking figure. Conan was with his army; how could he be here in Kordava?

Mordermi had systematically rooted out the White Rose after their riots against his rule—a task that was made the easier since the king knew most of their leadership personally. Not all of the underground organization had been arrested. Santiddio had remained in communication with those in Kordava who yet carried on despite Mordermi's persecution of his former allies. It was to these men that Conan looked for help.

Near the turning of an alley that pressed between dank walls at scarcely shoulder's breadth, Conan paused beside a low door, knocked carefully in a rhythmic pattern. A voice made a low muttering from the other side. Conan made a similar response. The door cracked open, and they slid inside.

A score of men and women were gathered in the dingy room beyond. There were crowded rows of filthy bunks, and beneath the low ceiling the air was sour with the stench of unwashed bodies and stale hashish fumes. Those who waited here tonight were not habitués of this sort of crib. Alert faces studied the two newcomers, and a casual glance noted a profusion of weapons ready to hand. Conan recognized about half of them. Voices murmured.

"Welcome back to the Pit, Conan," their leader greeted him. "Santiddio told me you were to come, but I didn't believe until now. The others were not told the reason for this gathering. I take few chances—else none of us would be here."

Conan returned their stares. These were a different breed from the followers of the White Rose that he remembered. The faces of these men and women were tight and bitter; there was none of the camaraderie and bright self-importance of the White Rose of Rimanendo's reign. This was not a debating society; these were dangerous fighters. Conan approved of them.

"The less you know, the better," Conan addressed them. "You know who I am, so you know I wouldn't be here without reason. I want a riot before the palace gate by the next hour. I need it to look good, and I need it to hold their attention. Make them turn out the guard, then get away as best you can. Is there anything more to tell you?"

The room remained silent. The White Rose had outgrown its youth—those who survived.

"There's another exit that leads topside," their leader directed Conan. "You've got your riot."

Not long after that, Conan and Destandasi crouched in the shadow of a doorway, watching the open court that separated the royal palace from the surrounding buildings. The mist grew denser as the moon set, and the interval of intense darkness that men call the hour of the wolf closed upon the city. Guards shivered at their posts atop the fortress walls, silently bemoaning the fact that they must stand sentinel duty even though the unfeeling stone flesh of the Final Guard was presence enough to defend the palace and indeed the entire city from any foe.

Conan tried to recall the exact posting of the guards. There was a chance that the routine had been changed since the army was under his command. With the impending battle, sentries may well have been doubled; sleepless soldiers might loiter in the night. But he had to reach the tower undetected, and the only way for them was to go over the wall.

Shouts pierced the silence from the main gate of the fortress. Conan, who waited beneath the walls opposite to the disturbance, could discern the wan glow of flames from that quarter, turning the fog opalescent. Dimly he could hear the words they shouted to those who stood guard at the tyrant's threshold.

"Soldiers of Zingara! Why do you serve the tyrant who has betrayed his people!"

"Whose brothers will his demons butcher next!"

"The army of liberation has come! Will you kill your brothers to preserve a tyrant!"

"Throw down your weapons! It is you who are slaves!"

"Come over to us! Join your brothers to depose the tyrant!"

"Death to the tyrant! Death to Mordermi!"

By now the answering shouts from the soldiers at the gate drowned out the uproar in the square beyond. From the flickering light, Conan guessed they must have fired a building. In the fortress, the garrison was turning out to quell the riot. All eyes would be drawn toward the disturbance before the gate.

Conan judged that the diversion was having the desired effect. "Here we go," he hissed to Destandasi.

Leaving the shelter of the doorway, they darted across the open space and into the shadow of the rear wall. In their dark cloaks, they would have been difficult to see even had a sentry been watching at that moment. Conan strained his ears, but heard no challenge from atop the wall.

From around his waist, the Cimmerian uncoiled a length of plaited silken rope, thin and light but immensely strong, with knots spaced along it to facilitate climbing. One end was tied to a small grapnel. Conan stepped back, cast the rope upward. The grapnel made a soft *chink* as it struck the rampart. Conan waited. The fog muffled all sound, and the riot before the main gate echoed crazily about the walls. Conan drew the rope taut, felt the grapnel scrape across the parapet, catch there.

He tested the grapnel's purchase with his weight. The rope was firmly anchored. "Are you ready?" he asked. The Cimmerian could swarm up the wall like a lizard—as once before he had scaled the Elephant Tower in Zamora—but his concern was for Destandasi. True, she had managed well enough after several practice climbs, but this was not a dry run.

"Go on," Destandasi whispered. They removed their cloaks for greater freedom of movement; Conan made a roll and thrust them into his swordbelt. Destandasi wore men's attire beneath her cloak—less restrictive for climbing than a woman's gown. In black trunk hose and loose shirt of black silk, her hair coiled upon her neck, she might have been a tall boy. The damp silk clung to her, so that Conan noticed that the breast over which her hair fell when she wore it as wont was somewhat smaller than the other.

"Are you ready?" she asked with icy inflection.

Conan went first, alert for sentries. He gained the rampart in an instant, it seemed, although the street was a good fifty feet below. He could see no one on the section of the wall. The diversion was working thus far. Steadying the rope, he watched Destandasi ascend—she was almost invisible in her black garments. She followed swiftly, gripping the knots in the slippery coil for purchase. The woman was lithe as a cat, and strong.

The palace proper stood within the *enceinte* of its fortress. The garrison barracks abutted the front wall. Between the rear wall and the palace buildings, the tower they must scale rose more than a hundred feet into the darkness. Originally the donjon, as the fortress expanded it was incorporated into the outer wall as a redoubt. Testament to its sturdiness, it was one of the few structures of old Kordava that had withstood the earthquake. With the walls of new Kordava protecting the city, the old fortress lost much of its defensive significance. Now Callidios had found a use for its tower.

Keeping low along the parapet, Conan and Destandasi reached the base of the tower without being seen. The uproar at the gate seemed to be spreading into the streets now, as the guard turned out to drive away the rioters. Moreover, a faint grayness stole through the sky in the east. Their time was growing short.

From the rampart to the summit of the tower rose a stone face of well over another fifty feet of height. The massive walls of the tower were unbroken for most of its height—near the base, the thickness of the walls must have been tremendous—although a few balistraria pierced the stone toward the top. Destandasi might conceivably wriggle through one of these; Conan, never. They must enter from the tower roof.

Conan cast his grapnel, drew the line taut—then cursed as the grapnel slid free and came spinning down upon the coiling rope. He made a second cast. This time the metal hooks held. Rapidly the Cimmerian clambered up the silken cord. He gained the roof of the tower, gazed quickly around.

Nothing moved atop the tower. Conan had assumed that Callidios would not permit sentries here—they would have had to pass through his secret chamber to reach the roof—and would trust to posting guards at the base of the tower stairs far below.

He turned to hold the rope for Destandasi. Watching her ascent, it was only some primitive instinct that warned him of danger in time.

A pool of darkness marked the steps that gave onto the tower roof. Up from the blackness lunged the jet figure of one of the Final Guard.

Conan hissed a warning, flung himself away from its

196

attack. An obsidian blade slammed into the parapet where he had stood an instant gone—narrowly missing the silken cord. The swordblade, had it have been forged or carven of any natural substance, would have shattered into fragments. Instead, it clove a gash into the stone of the parapet.

Conan backed away, sword in hand out of reflex. He had to draw the creature away from the rope until Destandasi had time to descend to the rampart again. The creature of living stone advanced upon him boldly. It had nothing to fear from Conan; presumably it was only the warrior's soul buried within its demon flesh that impelled it to go through the ritual of fencing with him, when it could as easily have rushed the Cimmerian and torn him apart in its hands.

Destandasi clambered over the parapet, her white face a ghostly blur in the night as she witnessed the unequal combat.

"Get away!" Conan warned with a curse. There was no safety below, but here there was certain death.

The creature turned to look upon this second intruder. Destandasi recoiled in horror. Her hand struck the silken cord, dislodging the grapnel. She caught at it as it slipped, but her fingers were clumsy. The rope plummeted away into the darkness.

Conan, as an armed opponent, drew the stone guardian's attention more so than an unarmed girl. The demon again made for the Cimmerian. Conan tried to parry a blow, almost lost his sword from the force of the blow. He felt the open space of the crenel at his back, and rolled beneath the next blow, instead of stepping back into space.

Destandasi uttered a piercing cry. It might have been an incoherent scream of fright, but there seemed to be syllables and cadence. Conan felt a tugging in his brain, but could not recognize the tongue, if such it was.

As Conan flung himself past the stone warrior, the creature

pivoted from the edge of the parapet to face the Cimmerian once again. As it raised its blade and started forward, leathery sails detached themselves from the darkness and flapped full into the demon's face.

Bats. A score of them suddenly. Attacking the head and face of the stone warrior. Their teeth and claws could not tear its invulnerable flesh, but the sudden frenzy of their attack drew the creature's attention for an instant.

Conan seized that instant. The creature's back was to the crenel, as he had stood a moment before. Conan lunged forward, thrust the point of his broadsword into the jet-armored chest with all his strength. The heavy blade bent under the impact.

The stone devil was driven backward by the blow. Overbalanced, it rocked back through the crenel. Arms clawed for support, as it toppled backward from the parapet. It fell silently.

From the street a hundred feet below, a jarring crash seemed to vibrate through the tower itself.

Conan glanced over the parapet, but could see nothing in the darkness far below. "If that didn't kill the devil, let's hope he takes his time climbing back. Crom! That's drawn their attention! It won't be long before they wonder how the thing came to fall off the tower."

He hastened to the steps that led below. "Those bats," he wondered. "They came in answer to your call."

"It was fortunate they did," Destandasi said. "Not many animals *remember*. There were these in reach of my cry who still do."

"This must be what we seek," Conan considered. "Callidios wouldn't trust human guardians—they might pry into his secret. Instead he left one of his devils to stand guard here."

"I pray there are no others."

"Callidios may have figured that one would be enough

to guard his chamber. If there are others, I think they would have attacked together."

Conan had been cautiously examining the darkened chamber beyond the landing. With a curse he abruptly threw himself across the chamber, racing for the door that opened to the steps below. The Cimmerian's keen ears had caught the scuff of booted feet ascending from below.

He stationed himself beside the door. It was certain to be locked, and Callidios would entrust the key to no one, Conan felt certain. If the door opened, then the person who entered would be Callidios—and Conan would kill him in that instant.

Instead there came a cautious knock. This was repeated, then was a soft call: "Callidios? Are you within?" When there came no answer, a hand tentatively tried the bolt. It was locked. The footfalls retreated quickly.

"Bad luck," Conan growled. "They'll fetch Callidios now. He won't be fool enough to come through that door by himself. When they find that rope on the rampart, the trail will lead straight to here."

In addition to the lock, the tower door might be secured from inside by means of a heavy timber. Conan set the bar into the iron brackets. It would hold for a while; the tower was designed to withstand a siege.

The shadows that spilled from the steps onto the landing were growing pale now. Conan squinted through a balistraria, saw that daylight was at hand. Santiddio would be on the march by now. Marching to his doom, if they failed him here.

"Well, what are we looking for?" Conan wanted to know. He groped for an oil lamp, struck fire and got it alight. He held the lamp high and examined the chamber they had gone to such pains to break into.

Conan had seen more than he cared of the inside of sorcerer's secret chambers, so that he knew what to expect to some extent. Withal, the interior of Callidios' chamber went counter to anything he had envisioned. The room was a shambles, a charnel house.

Strewn throughout the chamber with no more order than a child scatters her dolls about were human cadavers in every stage of decomposition. A mummy sprawled stiffly in a pile of tattered wrappings; its case was filled with a tangle of dried bones—some mineralized, others with shreds of red flesh. A shelf held a number of human fetuses, floating in preserving fluid. A beautifully articulated skeleton hung from a hook against the wall. Beside it hung some desiccated horror that desert winds had seared. A mass of charred bones had been dumped in a pile on the floor. Next to it lay something that Conan first thought was a lifelike doll, then saw that it wasn't a doll.

Conan shook his head in disbelief. The air was heavy with the taint of decay and the spices and perfumes and oils that had preserved these dead with varying success. Intricate pentagrams were chalked upon the floor, then carelessly obliterated by spills and footprints. Charts and scrolls were spread amidst a litter of books upon a low table.

"A necromancer's den," Destandasi broke their stunned silence. "But is Kalenius among these?"

"Crom's devils! What madness is this!"

"It may be that Callidios seeks knowledge of hidden treasures. Perhaps he seeks to unveil the future. I think the Stygian told no lie when he said he had walked far down his chosen path."

Footsteps again climbed the steps from below. It was the tread of many men. The key turned the lock, drawing back the bolt. Conan, sword ready, waited.

The door pressed against the heavy timber bar, nudging it against the iron brackets. Cautiously at first, then forcefully when the door refused to open. The door, Conan judged, would hold against a battering ram for as long as they needed.

"Open the door and come out," Callidios cajoled. "If you do so immediately, you'll not be harmed. I respect resourceful men; I promise you a helmet of gold coins and safe passage to our borders."

The Stygian must have thought it was worth the try. When Conan made no reply, Callidios spoke in a different tone: "I think you are going to be very sorry now."

Confident that the door was secure, Conan turned to help Destandasi search. He would have to stand guard on the parapet, as well as watch the door; others could follow where they had scaled the tower.

"Kalenius might be any of these," he swore.

"But he must be here. Callidios wouldn't have given us his attention just now otherwise. The necromancer should be at his task even now—he knows the Final Guard must be ready to repel our attack."

Impatient, the Cimmerian wrenched the lid from a coffin and dumped a pile of earth onto the floor. A stone sarcophagus resisted his efforts for a moment, then slid open to reveal a drifting layer of rotted dust. Angrily Conan ripped the dry wrappings from the mummy he had seen at first glance, glared into the leathery face.

It had been too quiet on the other side of the door. Conan had heard men depart, assumed they had gone for a ram and axes. He kept a wary eye on the door while he searched through the necrotorium. He could hear faint scraping sounds at one point, but nothing further. Its mystery worried him; Callidios was devious.

Then, in a powerful voice he had not thought the Stygian possessed: "Kalenius! Step forth to your master and harken to my commands!"

Conan whirled. A sudden rattle of dry bones pattered to

the floor. It came from the mummy case.

Rising stiffly from beneath the litter of bones that had hidden him, a naked man climbed out of the mummy case. He might have been a sleeper rising from his bed, but for the chill stiffness of his flesh. King Kalenius, his physique imposing for all his advanced age at the time of his death, glared at them with eyes that flamed with a mockery of life.

"Kalenius!" the necromancer commanded. "I require the two warriors who bar passage to the entrance of my tower to break down this door and to slay the intruders within!"

The dead king uttered no sound, but Conan heard the sudden pounding of stone tread upon stone stair, rising swifly from below.

"Hurry, Destandasi," he advised grimly.

She was facing the walking dead thing, her back to Conan. "Watch the door!" Destandasi commanded. "On your life, don't turn to watch me! Only a few are permitted to enter the mysteries of Jhebbal Sag; it is dangerous for others even to look upon the secret symbols of power!"

Conan turned his head. As he did so, in the corner of his eye he saw Destandasi start to draw a figure in the air. Blue flame hovered where her finger passed. Conan wrenched his eyes away, as the priestess of a forgotten god began to chant in the unknown tongue that seemed to stir memories within him.

The door shuddered under a massive blow. Conan gripped his useless sword and waited. A second blow shook the stout iron brackets. Timbers groaned inward.

"So . . . much . . . power . . ." Destandasi dragged the words out. "Must . . . try . . . again . . ."

Dust sifted down from the stones of the doorway under the tremendous force of the blows that struck it. The timbers of the door were starting to buckle under the enormous stress. Conan saw a crack appear in one of them, then splinters popped out. A ripping of wood and iron bolts, and a stone fist smashed through the thick timbers. Fingers gripped the edges of the opening, tore out great hunks of splinters.

Another fist rammed through another timber. Stone hands clawed at the wood, wrenched away the entire space between. The door was disintegrating before his eyes. Conan looked for something to barricade the crumbling door—knowing it could only buy a few moments for them.

Behind him, a rattling sigh gushed forth, then the hollow jumbled sound that an unconscious body makes as it collapses unchecked. Destandasi moaned.

And Conan could hear these sounds because the thunderous destruction of the door had abruptly ceased.

An arm of black stone thrust motionlessly past the aperture. As Conan watched, it began to bend downward. He expected the attack to renew, but the arm slopped over like a jointless thing. The stone flesh began to crack and flow, dropping away to expose crumbling bone. Pieces struck the floor, melted, dried into dust.

Conan gagged at the overpowering scent of decay. He tore his eyes from the hideous disintegration, gaped anew. On the floor where King Kalenius had fallen, a mass of crawling decay ran in a pool from collapsing loops of bone.

Conan caught up the half-conscious girl and staggered for fresh air on the tower roof.

Pandemonium reigned in the fortress spread out below them. Where the Final Guard had been stationed along the walls, pools of black liquescence boiled in a frenzy of ages-pent decay. Soldiers milled in gibbering panic, as their invincible allies rotted into masses of horror before their eyes. Through the main gate, soldiers fled in mindless fear.

The situation along the walls of Kordava, where the main force of the Final Guard had been posted to meet the rebel army, was a repetition of what was happening in the fortress below. The hideous demise of their invulnerable warriors was totally demoralizing to Kordava's human defenders — most of whom had expected to watch a day of massacre from a safe vantage.

From the tower Conan could see his army marching into positions for the near hopeless battle they had been prepared to fight. Advance scouts were riding headlong back to their commanders — carrying the report that Mordermi's sorcerous army had been annihilated by a greater sorcery. Santiddio would lose no time in launching his attack now — nor would he likely meet with any resistance. Kordava saw the destruction of the Final Guard at the moment the rebel army approached as a clear sign from the gods that Mordermi's rule was doomed.

A shuffling step from behind him brought the Cimmerian around. The door had been torn apart. An arm could reach through the gap and release the bar.

Callidios' eyes had the glare of madness as they regarded Conan with hatred. The Stygian's lips writhed like snakes.

"So it was you, Cimmerian," he said in jerking syllables. "The pawn returns to the king. It's wrong that way, you know. You've killed me now. Mordermi only used me to control the Final Guard. Now they're gone, and Mordermi will kill me too."

"I mean to spare Mordermi the trouble," Conan snarled, raising his sword.

Callidios' mad eyes blazed, as he put his hand to his rapier hilt. Conan gave him time to draw his blade — the Cimmerian would have cut the Stygian down like a mad dog, but it was better that the sorcerer face him man to man. He wondered if Callidios could even fence; he had never seen him draw his weapon.

The Stygian's rapier cleared its scabbard. It seemed far too long a blade. Callidios lunged. His blade shot out for Conan's throat. No blade of steel, but a living serpent. From its tip, dripping fangs struck at his flesh.

Conan flung himself away, bringing up his own blade just in time to sever the serpent head. The head flew away. Callidios laughed crazily, bringing his serpent-blade behind him, then flicking it forward like a whip. Another snake's head snapped venomously for his flesh.

Conan slashed at the uncanny weapon, again severed its serpent body. The whiplike speed was more than any swordsman could parry for long.

"Keep your guard up, barbarian!" Callidios shrilled. "How long can you escape? The head returns with each blow, and its fangs are deadly. Keep dancing for me!"

Conan knew he could not keep this up very long. Again the serpent-blade lashed out, while the sorcerer pranced beyond the Cimmerian's reach. Conan cut through the blade even as its fangs brushed his chest.

Conan glanced quickly to see if there was a wound, saw the roll of their cloaks he had thrust in his swordbelt. His free hand tore the roll loose. He threw it as Callidios lunged.

The cloaks unfurled with a snap of black silk, billowing to ensnare the serpent-blade. Callidios howled, as the coiling blade tangled in the silk folds. Conan's broadsword struck in that moment, and the necromancer departed on the road from which he had recalled his slaves.

Beneath the cloaks, a reptillian frenzy heaved the folds. Conan smashed down with his boot. Kept smashing long after all movement had ceased.

Destandasi was arousing herself from her semi-consciousness. Slowly she came to her feet, regarded the Stygian's body. "So, it is ended." Her eyes held the shadow of the stresses she had endured in her struggle.

"There's still Mordermi," Conan said.

Mordermi was finished, he knew. Santiddio's entrance into Kordava had been more of a hero's welcome than an assault. It was no longer any question of defending the city against the rebels—Kordava belonged to the rebels. Few of

Mordermi's soldiers put up any resistance; some fled, some managed to surrender. The mob was massacring the rest.

Conan turned away in disgust. He had seen this spectacle and had not liked it better then.

"There's still Mordermi," he said.

They descended from the tower. At the threshold of the smashed door, Conan noted an indistinct patch of dust, almost impalpable, and a few bits of corroded metal that crumbled when he stepped on them.

The soldiers had virtually deserted the fortress. The few who remained were looting. The rumble of the mob was drawing near, and in a moment they would stream through the open gate.

They entered the palace unchallenged. Conan's blade was naked in his fist, but there were none here to stand and fight. The Final Guard had failed them, leaving them at the mercy of those whom they had oppressed; knowing what mercy to expect, they deserted Mordermi and fled.

Conan knew the way to Mordermi's private chambers. He kicked in the locked door and entered.

Mordermi was stuffing jewels from a large chest into an almoner, clearly disturbed that he must leave some choice gems behind. The king of Zingara wore dirty laborers' garments and a patched cloak. His hair had been powdered to a mouldy gray, and when he pulled the bloody bandage back down over his face, he would blend into the crowd well enough.

"You should have deserted with the rest of the rats," Conan told him. "Or does the rat-captain go down with his ship?"

Mordermi recovered nicely. "Well, Conan. Here already? I'd thought the press of well-wishers would delay your triumphal procession somewhat longer than this."

"Your well-wishers are about to start a new coronation revel just outside. You remember the last one? Of course, first there's the abdication ceremony.''

Mordermi swept off his masquerade bandages. ''That's why I'm relieved that you're here to take my surrender, Conan. I know I can count on you to deal fairly with me. You're a man of honor.''

''What makes you think you have anything to hope for in a fair deal, Mordermi? There's not rope enough to hang you for all of your crimes.''

''And this from the felon I saved from the gallows?'' Mordermi's voice was pained. ''I'd thought better of your gratitude than that, Conan. After all, we both have committed crimes which would hang us a hundred times over, if we were caught.''

''I've never betrayed a friend,'' Conan sneered.

''Mitra, if I could only undo all those tragic errors of judgment! You were right, Conan. I should have let you slay Callidios the night he sought us out. That Stygian poisoned my brain with his schemes and lies. I know now that he had some sort of hold over my thoughts—some spell or drug.''

''The only drug that poisoned your brain was your lust for power, Mordermi. You used Callidios just like you used all of us. The more power you had in your hands, the more you wanted to grasp, and when you had it all, you still kept reaching. I liked you, Mordermi, and I'd like to think that you were somebody worth liking once, before power poisoned you. But maybe you were poisoned all along, just waiting for the right moment to use your friends because their backs were all the easier to thrust your knife into when you were through with them.''

''That's quite a speech for you, Conan,'' Mordermi said with his easy grace. ''Santiddio was right, also: you are an altruist. All right then, call in your men and arrest me. I'll plead my case to the people.''

''What men?'' Conan jeered. ''The palace is deserted but

207

for us! Santiddio is leading the army into Kordava. Destandasi and I climbed over your wall this morning, so she could break Callidios' control over the Final Guard. You can thank what you did to Sandokazi for Destandasi's taking a hand. Did she trust you all the time that the noose was closing on her throat, Mordermi? Did you know she made the two of us promise not to kill you before she'd unlock our cell?''

But Conan in his rage had already said too much. The Cimmerian saw Mordermi's face change, his hand thrust against something beneath his ornate desk. Acting without thought, Conan yelled and lunged for Mordermi.

Behind him, the floor dropped open an instant after his feet left the tiles.

Destandasi, still dazed from her exorcism, had no chance to react to Conan's shout. Her outcry as she fell downward throught the trap was abruptly stilled.

Conan's leap carried him onto the desk, scattering the chest of jewels across the room. Mordermi, agile as ever, rolled away from the desk and from the Cimmerian's hurtling body. He was on his feet like an acrobat, rapier drawn, as Conan flung himself clear of the desk.

"I see you still favor the broadsword, barbarian," Mordermi smiled. "Shall I give you another lesson in swordplay?"

Conan in a rage sprang toward him—nearly taking Mordermi's lunge as he bored in on the man. He parried the lighter blade with just enough speed, then slashed for the extended arm. Mordermi retreated with a laugh.

The Cimmerian's wrath was too great for niceties of fencing. Mordermi sensed this and goaded him, confident that in a moment the Cimmerian would lose his head—rush in with a frenzy of slash and smash brawling. Then Mordermi would drill him.

Conan pressed him tirelessly, neither blade striking home. The Cimmerian's speed was too great for Mordermi to risk opening his guard in a counterattack, as he could safely have done with any normal swordsman of Conan's bulk and temperament. Mordermi had seen Conan's handiwork too often; he must play a waiting game and then strike true.

The noise of the crowd in the courtyard below was beginning to rattle the panes in the window. Mordermi realized that it was Conan, not he, who could win a waiting game. He must dispatch the berserk Cimmerian quickly, or escape would be impossible.

Suddenly Mordermi saw his chance, as Conan drove him back with another of his reckless slashes. As the heavier blade ripped past, Mordermi's riposte penetrated Conan's guard. The rapier should have pierced the Cimmerian's heart; instead, Conan twisted at the final instant, and the thin blade impaled the thick muscles that framed shoulder and axilla.

Conan grunted, and seized the outstretched wrist. A brutal twist, and Conan snapped the blade.

Mordermi surged backward, but the Cimmerian pinned his arm and the hand that still clutched the hilt of the broken rapier. Conan's swordarm came down, but it was the basket hilt, and not the blade, that smashed into Mordermi's face.

Dashed half-senseless, Mordermi was hurled to the floor. Standing over him, Conan contemptuously withdrew the broken rapier blade from his shoulder muscles, threw it across the room.

"So much for your gentleman's toy," he growled. "I could have finished you with a score of your stickpins in my hide!"

Mordermi's face was a bloody ruin, his nerve broken. "You swore you wouldn't kill me," he cringed. The Cimmerian, blood pouring from his shoulder, eyes murderous with rage, was not a reassuring sight.

"I won't kill you," Conan sneered. "Why would I have only fought to disarm you, if I didn't keep my word? I'm

209

a man of honor, Mordermi—you said it yourself.''

The roar of the mob shook the palace now. Conan could hear the smash of glass, the crash of doors being forced from the floor below. In a moment the mob would be surging through the palace. Conan had seen that before too.

He threw open the windows of Mordermi's chamber. A dozen feet below, hundreds of angry faces looked up at him. Rocks pelted through the aperture. The mob was in a bloodthirsty mood. They wanted vengeance after the Final Guard's reign of fear.

Conan hauled Mordermi to his feet, dragged him to the window. The mob saw movement there, and began to surge forward.

''Conan, what are you doing! You promised not to kill me!''

''I'm not going to kill you,'' Conan repeated. ''You said you would plead your case to the people. Well, I'm going to let you.''

Thrusting the frenzied king through the window, Conan dropped him to the waiting mob below. The screams that lasted for some while afterward reassured the Cimmerian that the short fall had not killed Mordermi.

By the time Santiddio reached the palace, the mob of looters had carried away all but the stripped walls. And by then Conan had descended into the pit beneath Mordermi's trap, brought up the body that lay impaled at the bottom. Conan sat beside the body, leaning against the wall, bandages covering his arm, a cloak spread over Destandasi. He was not paying close attention to Santiddio's words.

''She will be remembered as a heroine of the liberation,'' he was concluding. ''All Kordava knows the story of how you two saved our land from the Final Guard, how you freed Zingara from Mordermi's tyranny.''

He gestured toward the open window. Cheers instead of angry shouts resounded from below now. And one of the cheers was the chant: "Conan! Conan! Conan!"

"You're a hero, Conan," Santiddio told him. "Say that you will accept the crown of Zingara, and the people will proclaim you their king in this moment!"

The crown had been found in one of Mordermi's hidden coffers—preserved from the mob out of reverence for tradition. Santiddio held it out to Conan.

"Crom's devils, Santiddio! Take that out of my sight!"

"I know how you must feel, Conan," Santiddio said. "Both of us have lost good friends; I have lost two sisters. But think upon it. Zingara must have a king. The people love you. You are the greatest hero of the age. Take the crown!"

"Santiddio," Conan's voice was grim. "In the morning I take a canoe to carry Destandasi back to her sanctuary."

"You'll change your mind."

"I will not change my mind."

Santiddio held the crown in his hands, thinking. The procession through Kordava at the head of his army had been a glorious moment, making up for much pain and sorrow. And some of the cheers that floated through the palace window cried out "Santiddio! Santiddio!"

Conan's eyes were on him. Santiddio flushed.

"If you will not change your mind, then I will accept the crown from the people myself. Zingara must have a king, until a new constitution can be established."

"I will not change my mind," Conan repeated. "Not until I know whether it is the man who corrupts the power, or the power that corrupts the man."

About the Author

KARL EDWARD WAGNER is one of the most talented of the younger fantasy writers, and best known for his heroic fantasy saga of the mystical swordsman Kane. Born in 1945, he maintains a deep interest in and knowledge of fiction from the pulp era. Prior to becoming a full-time writer, Wagner was a practicing psychiatrist and M.D. He lives in Chapel Hill, North Carolina, with his wife, Barbara.

CONAN

☐ 11481-4	**CONAN, #1**	$2.95
☐ 11453-9	**CONAN OF CIMMERIA, #2**	$2.95
☐ 11863-1	**CONAN THE FREEBOOTER, #3**	$2.95
☐ 11597-7	**CONAN THE WANDERER, #4**	$2.95
☐ 11858-5	**CONAN THE ADVENTURER, #5**	$2.95
☐ 11585-3	**CONAN THE BUCCANEER, #6**	$2.95
☐ 11586-1	**CONAN THE WARRIOR, #7**	$2.95
☐ 11589-6	**CONAN THE USURPER, #8**	$2.95
☐ 11590-X	**CONAN THE CONQUEROR, #9**	$2.95
☐ 11471-7	**CONAN THE AVENGER, #10**	$2.95
☐ 11472-5	**CONAN OF AQUILONIA, #11**	$2.95
☐ 11623-X	**CONAN OF THE ISLES, #12**	$2.95
☐ 11716-3	**CONAN: THE FLAME KNIFE**	$2.95
☐ 11628-0	**CONAN THE MERCENARY**	$2.95
☐ 11479-2	**CONAN THE SWORDSMAN**	$2.95
☐ 11480-6	**CONAN: THE SWORD OF SKELOS**	$2.95